SQUEEZE PLAY

Alanna Taylor was a gorgeous female—but that wasn't why Skye Fargo grabbed her. He grabbed her because she had three gunmen drawing a bead on him—and she was his only shield.

He heard her gasp with surprise when he yanked her off her horse and dropped with her on the ground with her luscious body on top of him. In another spot he would have enjoyed the warm pressure of her full breasts and spread-out thighs. But now all he was interested in was the cold feel of his Colt .45 as he drew it from his holster.

He got off a quick shot that drowned out Alanna's screams, and sent one of the gunmen flying backwards.

One down and two to go, thought the Trailsman. And after that, he'd have his chance to deal with Alanna as she so richly deserved. . . .

Ⓞ SIGNET WESTERNS BY JON SHARPE   (0451)

RIDE THE WILD TRAIL

WILDCAT WAGON

by

Jon Sharpe

A SIGNET BOOK

NEW AMERICAN LIBRARY

PUBLISHER'S NOTE

This book is a work of fiction. Names, characters, places, and incidents either are the product of the author's imagination or are used fictitiously, and any resemblance to actual persons, living or dead, events, or locales is entirely coincidental.

Copyright © 1988 by Jon Sharpe

All rights reserved

The first chapter of this book previously appeared in *Colorado Robber,* the seventy-fifth volume in this series.

SIGNET TRADEMARK REG. U.S. PAT. OFF. AND FOREIGN COUNTRIES
REGISTERED TRADEMARK—MARCA REGISTRADA
HECHO IN CHICAGO, U.S.A.

SIGNET, SIGNET CLASSIC, MENTOR, ONYX, PLUME,
MERIDIAN and NAL BOOKS are published by NAL PENGUIN INC.,
1633 Broadway, New York, New York 10019

First Printing, April, 1988

1 2 3 4 5 6 7 8 9

PRINTED IN THE UNITED STATES OF AMERICA

The Trailsman

Beginnings . . . they bend the tree and they mark the man. Skye Fargo was born when he was eighteen. Terror was his midwife, vengeance his first cry. Killing spawned Skye Fargo, ruthless, cold-blooded murder. Out of the acrid smoke of gunpowder still hanging in the air, he rose, cried out a promise never forgotten.

The Trailsman they began to call him all across the West: searcher, scout, hunter, the man who could see where others only looked, his skills for hire but not his soul, the man who lived each day to the fullest, yet trailed each tomorrow. Skye Fargo, the Trailsman, the seeker who could take the wildness of a land and the wanting of a woman and make them his own.

1860, south of Pikes Peak, where the Sangre de Cristo Mountains spill from Colorado into the turbulent territory called New Mexico . . .

1

"Put that thing down, honey. It might go off," the big man with the lake-blue eyes said, his voice calm.

"It will go off, and put a hole right through you, unless you do what I say," the girl snapped, and the big man's eyes narrowed as he peered hard at her. He saw light-brown hair and eyes to match, a small, straight nose in a pretty face with soft cheeks and nicely curved lips. But the eyes were as determined as the thrust of her jaw.

"Get off the horse," she said, and he eyed the heavy, breech-loading Henry leveled at him. She held the rifle without a quiver and the big man slowly swung one leg from the saddle and landed lightly on the balls of his feet. The rifle followed him, he saw, and he cursed silently. The trip had been pleasantly peaceful and easy riding until the girl had exploded out of the trees, the rifle already held on him.

"You're too damn pretty to be playing highwayman, honey," he offered.

"I'm not playing highwayman," she snapped back, and he let his eyes roam across a tan shirt covering smallish breasts, a small waist, and trim legs in tight Levi's, and he returned his gaze to the determined, tight face.

"Then you're making some kind of mistake," he said.

"No mistake. You're the Trailsman. . . .Skye Fargo," she countered.

"One for you," Fargo said with some surprise.

"And you're on your way to General Taylor to break trail for his wagon train."

"Two for you," Fargo grunted, and felt surprise again.

"I'm going on that train. I'm going to be part of it and you're going to see to it."

"The hell I am, honey."

"You'll see to it, or else," she said tightly, and Fargo saw the big old Henry still didn't waver. But he felt the irritation spiraling inside him.

"I've heard enough, girlie. You move on before I get real mad," he said, and started to turn back to the Ovaro. The shot exploded and he felt the rush of air as the bullet almost grazed his cheek. Instinctively, he twisted, went down on one knee, and reached for the six-gun at his side.

"Don't, dammit," her voice snapped out, and he halted, his hand frozen in midair, and he eyed the big Henry aimed directly at his chest. Slowly, he drew his hand back from the butt of the Colt and pushed to his feet, his eyes now cold as a lake in midwinter.

"What are you all about?" Fargo frowned.

"What I'm about is being part of that wagon train, and I'll pay you three hundred dollars to make that happen," she said.

Fargo's lips pursed at the offer. "That's a lot of money," he remarked. "But I can't make you part of anything."

"Yes, you can. Taylor needs you. He'll go along with whatever you ask. You promise to include me, that's all."

"Sorry, I can't do that."

"Dammit, you can. You include me or you'll never break another trail for anybody," she said, her voice rising.

"How'll that help you?" Fargo questioned calmly.

"He'll have to get somebody else and I'll get them

to include me," she tossed back, and Fargo's eyes peered into her. She was not as hard as she tried to make herself out to be. That showed in the whiteness of her knuckles as she gripped the rifle, and in the tiny lines of nervousness that touched the corners of her mouth. There was desperation behind her hardness.

He put reasonableness into his voice. "You're being real dumb, honey. I could agree now and not mean one damn word of it. Talk's cheap."

"You wouldn't do that. You're not the kind. You'd stay by your word."

"How do you know that about me?"

"I know, just leave it at that."

"How'd you know it was me riding the road?"

"I knew you rode a real handsome Ovaro and you were due," she answered. Fargo took in the rifle again. It hadn't wavered an inch and her knuckles were still white. "Well, will you give me your word?" she pressed.

He let thoughts whirl inside him for a long moment. "Looks as though you and that big old Henry don't give me much choice but to do what you want," he said with a resigned shrug. He saw her breasts push tiny points into the shirt with the deep rush of breath she let hiss from her.

"Then I'll look for you in Claysville," she said, and backed the brown mare away from him without lowering the rifle.

"Wait," Fargo said. "Aren't you going to tell me anything about yourself?"

"When the time comes," the girl said, and continued to back away. Suddenly, she yanked the mare to the left and sent the horse racing into the trees.

Fargo waited for a few moments and listened to her riding up through the hillside. When the sound of her died away, he swung onto the Ovaro and turned the horse up through the trees. He felt the anger simmering inside him as he quickly picked up her trail, hoofprints fresh and clear in the soft ground, leaves pressed down, grass and moss clearly marked with the edges of the hooves. She'd not only threatened him and almost shot his ear off and tried to force him into wild promises, but she seemed to know more about him than she ought. Now it'd be his turn to demand answers, he vowed as he followed her prints where she'd made a wide circle up a gentle slope, stayed in the trees, and finally started down the other side to a road below.

Fargo stayed higher on the slope and caught sight of her, moved the Ovaro forward to stay above her and slightly behind as she continued down the slope. She rode slowly, absorbed in her own thoughts. Fargo took the lariat from the fork swell and lifted the rope above his head. He sent the rope into an easy, graceful spin, pushed the Ovaro a dozen feet closer to his target, and sent the lariat spinning through the air. She suddenly sensed danger and looked up just in time to see the loop coming down to fall over her. Fargo pulled and the lasso tightened around her, and she gave a small shriek as she came out of the saddle, the cry turning to an oath when she landed on her rear in a clump of brush.

Fargo rode up quickly, pulling her to her feet with the lariat. Arms pinned to her sides, she spit fury at him as he dismounted. "You bastard," she said. "You gave me your word."

"Try again. All I said was that you didn't give me much choice at the point of a gun," Fargo said. "Now you're going to talk, honey." He scooped up the Henry, which had fallen to the ground, before he loosened the coil of the lasso around her. "You've a name. Start with that," he growled.

"Sally Jamison," she muttered, and rubbed her rear with one hand. "You didn't have to be so damn rough."

"Same to you, honey," Fargo said. "How come you know so much about me?"

"General Taylor's been talking a lot about your coming."

"That doesn't explain everything you said."

"Tim Greenspun," she said. "My folks were good friends with him. He used to talk about you often."

Fargo's eyes stayed on her as he considered her reply. He'd broken many a trail for Tim Greenspun, and Tim had come to know him better than most. He decided to accept the answer, as far as it went. "Let's have the rest of it," he said. "Why do you have to be part of General Taylor's wagon train?"

"That's my business for now."

"Damn, you've more brass than a bar rail."

"I'll tell you when the time comes for it," she said.

Fargo stared at her. Without the big Henry she was hardly formidable, a small girl with a neat figure that matched the pleasant prettiness of her face. But her light-brown eyes still blazed determination, and he shook his head at her.

"There won't be any time, Sally Jamison," he said. "Get on your horse and ride."

"You saying you won't help me?" she flung at him, and he heard the incredulousness in his own voice.

"Help you? You're lucky if I don't turn you over my knee and fan your tail!" He emptied the shells from the rifle and tossed it at her. She caught it deftly with one hand and, with something close to a flounce, spun and pulled herself into the saddle. She paused to glare back at him, her light-brown eyes blazing.

"You'll take that wagon train out and I'll be part of it," she said. "Or you'll be sorry, Skye Fargo."

"*Git!*" he barked, and she dug her heels into the brown mare and sent the horse galloping downhill. He watched her go till she was out of sight in the foliage before he returned to the saddle. He turned and rode back down the other side of the hill to the road. The incident had been as strange as unexpected. Maybe she was just a wild, headstrong hellion all caught up in her own wild concerns. Maybe he'd seen the last of her, he told himself, and grimaced as he knew it was a hollow wish. She was too full of fire to just back off from whatever it was that drove her. But maybe he could meet with General Morton Taylor and get the wagon train rolling without delay. The man had contacted him by letter and enclosed the kind of up-front money only a fool could ignore. Of course, he had some questions to ask the general before he took the job, Fargo reflected. But he couldn't think of answers that would make him turn down the kind of money offered.

The Trailsman reached the road and put the Ovaro into a trot. Claysville was still a good distance away, west of Spanish Peak in Colorado Territory, and he was grateful for the road that cut through the heavy forest on both sides. He'd gone perhaps another mile when the road took a slow incline upward, and he reached the top to see the road stretching out in an almost straight line. He also saw the lone rider coming toward him, and his hand went to the Colt at his side. The rider came closer and he took in long black hair, thick and free-flowing black eyes, an aquiline nose, a full, wide mouth, and everything held together by smoothly sensuous olive skin. She wore a yellow shirt and black riding britches, and he saw somewhat long breasts that swayed beautifully in unison as she rode. Her beauty—and it was surely that—seemed a product of two cultures, one north of the border, the other south.

The young woman came to a halt and surveyed him with a cool appraisal that bordered on arrogance, but she didn't quite mask the appreciation in it. "Skye Fargo, the Trailsman," she said, and her voice was low, almost husky.

"Not again," Fargo bit out.

"I beg your pardon." She frowned.

"Nothing. Go on."

"You are the Trailsman, right?" the young woman said, and he nodded.

"How'd you know?" he asked.

"I was told you rode a really magnificent Ovaro," she said. "And you're expected today."

He let his eyes take in the slow swell of the longish breasts that formed fully rounded cups at the bottoms. "I hope you're the real welcoming committee," he remarked.

"I wouldn't exactly say that," she answered coolly.

"What would you exactly say?" Fargo pushed at her.

"No wagon train," she snapped.

"Want to run that past again."

"You're not going to break trail for that wagon train," she said. "It's not going out."

Fargo's lips pursed as he studied her. "Same melody, different words," he grunted.

"What's that mean?"

"Never mind. Tell me more," Fargo said.

"I'll double what General Taylor has offered you. All you have to do is take it and leave," she said.

"That'd be a powerful lot of money," Fargo said.

"I know that, but that wagon train must not go out," she replied. "Without you, it won't."

"He could find somebody else," Fargo suggested.

"Not like you, and he needs the very best," she answered. "And it'd take a long time to find someone else." She met his curious stare with an upward tilt of her chin. "I've the money with me. You can just take it and go back."

"If I say no, honey, what, then?" Fargo asked.

"You're a dead man, Skye Fargo. One way or the other, you are not taking out that wagon train," she answered.

"Why not? What's all this to you?" Fargo questioned.

"That is none of your concern," the beautiful young woman said, and Fargo probed into her coolly lovely face, which wore both peasant sensuousness and aristocratic hauteur. She was as different from Sally Jamison as her demands were.

"I want some reasons, honey," he said. "You could give me your name, too."

"No reasons. No name. Just take the money and leave," she said. "You can leave alive and richer, or dead and poorer."

"You've a way of putting things, don't you?" Fargo smiled and she shrugged, her breasts pressing into the yellow shirt for an instant. "Just how do you figure I'll be dead?"

"There are three guns trained on you this very moment," she said. Fargo kept his face impassive and his eyes on her. "I wouldn't like to see that happen. You're still young and good-looking and I'm sure there are lots of ladies still waiting for you."

"I sure hope so."

"Then you'll take the money and leave?"

He kept his eyes steady on her, refusing to give her the satisfaction of looking past her into the trees that lined the road. But his thoughts raced and something told him she wasn't making hollow threats. She didn't seem the kind for that, and the thick woods could hide a lot more than three men. He turned words in his mind. If she had three gunmen trained on him, he wanted them out in the open. "You know what I think, honey?" He smiled. "I think you're full of shit."

He watched her black eyes grow blacker. "You're making a mistake, Fargo," she warned icily.

"And you're as dumb as you are beautiful if you think I'm going to just believe you," he slid at her, and saw her frown as she considered his reply.

"Yes, perhaps that is asking too much of someone

16

such as you,'' she said. She raised her left arm into the air and brought it down again slowly.

Fargo looked past her to where the three riders carefully pushed out of the trees. He sized up the three men immediately as they halted, keeping distance between themselves. Two held rifles, raised and aimed, and the third held a five-shot, single-action Joslyn army revolver. All three were pickup gun hands, none carrying a real gunfighter's weapons and each too tense. But there were three and they had their firepieces aimed. He needed a few seconds, just enough to make them hesitate.

''Satisfied?'' the young woman asked with an edge of cold triumph.

Fargo shrugged. ''Guess so,'' he said. ''I never was one for getting myself shot. You say you've the money with you?''

''Yes, right here,'' the young woman said, and drew an envelope from her shirt pocket.

''Guess you made yourself a deal,'' Fargo said, and moved the Ovaro toward her horse, a dark-gray gelding with black spots on its rump.

She allowed a tiny smile to curl the edges of her wide but attractive mouth. ''I'm glad you're not as difficult as I'd heard you were,'' she said as he halted alongside her.

He started to reach out for the envelope when suddenly the casual movement changed into a lightning-like lunge. He closed one hand around her forearm and yanked, and she flew from her horse into his arms. He let himself go backward from the Ovaro with her and heard her curse of surprise and anger. He cast a quick glimpse at the three gunmen and saw they looked on with the moment of hesitation he wanted, unable to get a clear shot and uncertain whether to risk firing at all.

Fargo rolled when he hit the ground with the girl and only pushed her aside when he reached the heavy brush at the edge of the road. He yanked at his Colt while she half-fell, half-ran through the brush, and he took quick aim at the man with the Joslyn army pistol. He fired and the man flew backward from the saddle as though he'd been hit by a huge, invisible baseball bat.

"Shoot, damn you, shoot," he heard the young woman scream, and the two remaining riders dived from their horses as Fargo fired again. He saw his first shot graze the shirt collar of one of the men as he dived to the ground, and Fargo drew deeper into the brush, holding back another shot as the two figures disappeared into the trees.

"Get him. Go after him," the girl ordered from the edge of the treeline as she stuffed the envelope back in her shirt. Fargo half-rose, shook the low branch of a tree, and dived onto his stomach as four shots whistled over his head to slam into tree trunks.

The Trailsman stayed on his stomach, reloaded the Colt, and kept his head down as he let his ears become his eyes. The two men were making their way through the brush toward him and he followed their paths by the rustle of leaves and the sound of branches being pressed back. One moved away from the other, he detected, a second path of sound opening to his right. They were attempting an encircling movement, aware that their quarry had to be somewhere in the brush in front of them.

Fargo carefully let his long legs stretch out and positioned himself. Once he fired, he'd reveal his position and one or the other would immediately send a fusillade of hot lead his way. He grimaced and raised his hand with the big Colt in it. He knew what he'd have to do to strike and stay alive after it.

Fargo peered through the leaves and the brush and saw the man come into view, crawling carefully, the rifle held in front of him and ready to fire. He listened again, let his wild-creature hearing pick out sounds.

18

The second one was not more than a few yards to the right of the first. Fargo let the man come closer and waited until the searcher halted. The man had a narrow, tight face, and as he stayed in place and swept the brush to his left with the rifle at his shoulder, Fargo waited, letting him come around to the center of his circle. The sound of pulling back the hammer would seem loud as a dropped stone in the silence and Fargo's thumb rested on the hammer and he waited another ten seconds. He pulled it back and fired almost in one motion and the bullet grazed the side of the rifle barrel and smashed into the man's face. Fargo flung himself sideways instantly as the shower of red spray exploded to coat the leaves. He heard the explosion of bullets that thudded into the ground where he'd lain, and he rolled again as two more bullets plowed into the soil closer to him.

Landing against the base of a tree trunk, he stayed flat, skidded himself in a half-circle, and spotted the brush moving to his right. The third man still hunted for him and Fargo caught a glimpse of a hat that vanished behind a clump of tall brush. Another sound suddenly interrupted, the sharp tattoo of hoofbeats racing away. The girl had decided to take her horse and bolt, Fargo grunted, and he saw the brush suddenly quiver. The third man had made the same decision.

Fargo rose, drove powerful legs through the brush toward the road, and reached the edge of the trees in time to see the man vault onto his horse.

"Hold it right there, mister," Fargo shouted. The man half-spun in the saddle, fired a wild shot from the rifle, dug heels into the horse's side, and began to race away. Fargo took a moment to aim. He wanted the man alive and able to answer questions. He fired and saw the man fall forward, drop the rifle, and twist his body in pain as the bullet slammed into his shoulder. But he managed to cling to the horse's mane and prevent himself from falling, and Fargo cursed as he ran to where the Ovaro waited. He leapt onto the horse and bent low in the saddle as he sent the pinto into a gallop. The fleeing assailant stayed on the road and Fargo closed quickly, seeing the man glance back in pain and fright as he tried desperately to coax more speed from his horse. But Fargo drew almost abreast of him in minutes and the man surprised him by suddenly reining up. His horse reared as it was yanked to a halt and Fargo skidded past before he could bring the pinto to a halt and he saw the man had slid from the horse's rump to the ground and started into the trees on foot.

"Come back here, you damn fool," Fargo shouted, and leapt to the ground, the Colt in his hand. He heard the man crashing through the woods and ran after him and quickly spotted his quarry as the man half-stumbled, half-ran, one arm hanging loosely. The Trailsman closed in on the fleeing figure, dropped down when the man suddenly whirled and fired three wild shots from a six-gun in his right hand. As the man turned and started to run again, Fargo rose, raised the Colt, aimed, and fired again. The man's gasp of pain came loud and clear as he fell and Fargo ran forward, reached the figure as the man pulled himself to his feet again, swayed, and fell to the ground. The second shot had gone clean through his other shoulder, Fargo saw as he reached down and yanked the man up against the base of a tree. He kicked the man's gun away from where it had fallen.

"I need a doc. I'm bleeding to death," the man groaned.

"Talk, first," Fargo rasped. "Who was she?

"I don't know. She never gave us her name."

"If you're lying you'll need an undertaker, not a doctor," Fargo said.

"Not lyin'," the man said. "She hired us three days ago."

"And you don't know anything more about her," Fargo pressed.

"Nothin'," the man said. "Christ, I hurt bad. Get me to a doc."

"Claysville's a long ride," Fargo said.

"In my saddlebag . . . bandages," the man gasped, and Fargo holstered the Colt and strode to the horse. He had lifted the flap of the saddlebag when he caught the faint sound, a rush of breath from sudden painful exertion. He dropped before he whirled, and the shot grazed his head and slammed into the saddlehorn. The horse bolted, but Fargo had the Colt out of its holster in a split-second motion and he fired at the figure against the tree. The shot slammed into the man's abdomen and he seemed to erupt in a shower of entrails. The gun in his hand fell to the ground and Fargo saw the opened buttons of the shirt where he'd had the second gun hidden inside.

"Goddamn fool," Fargo muttered, and rose to his feet. If the man had known more, he'd not be telling it now, Fargo grunted silently and walked to the Ovaro. He climbed onto the horse, slowly rode away, and felt the frown that dug into his brow. A nice, peaceful day had suddenly become not at all peaceful. A nice, simple job of breaking trail for a wagon train had suddenly become not at all simple. Two lovely young woman had threatened to kill him—one if he didn't take the wagon train out, the other if he did. It was less than a promising beginning, Fargo half-smiled. But it promised not to be dull, either.

2

Fargo found still another surprise in store for him when he reined up in front of the Claysville hotel. He had just ridden through the town in the gathering dusk and found Claysville a noisy place filled with wagons, pack mules, splintery buildings, two dance halls, and red clay dirt that churned into mud underfoot and covered everything with a fine reddish silt. But the Claysville hotel had a white fence around it bordered with red carnations, tidy, neatly painted shutters that made it look prim and proper and as misplaced as a schoolgirl in a whorehouse. He tethered the Ovaro to the hitching post and strolled into the hotel, where he surveyed an equally neat waiting room with doilies on the somewhat worn, stuffed chairs. A thin, elderly desk clerk looked up at him patiently.

Following the instructions in the letter inside his jacket, Fargo replied to the question in the man's glance. "Name's Fargo, Skye Fargo. There might be a message here for me," he said.

"There is," a voice said to his right, and Fargo turned to see a tall woman, brown hair pulled severely back, a very proper buttoned-to-the-neck white dress on a narrow figure that flattened her bustline. She had brown eyes and even features that might have been attractive if they weren't held in so primly, lips thinned out more than they actually were, her expression determinedly austere. "A note from General Taylor," she said, and took a small envelope from the mail slots behind the front desk and handed it to him. She looked on as he tore it open and read the authoritative handwriting.

> Having a dinner party at my home on Thursday the 5th. Expect you'll be here by then.
>
> General Morton Taylor

Fargo let his lips purse as he pushed the note into his pocket. "When's Thursday the fifth?" he asked.

"Tomorrow," the woman answered, and Fargo nodded. He glanced at the desk clerk.

"Then I'll be taking a room for the night," Fargo said. "I've either an invitation or a command. I'm not sure which."

"Give Mr. Fargo room four," the woman said, and Fargo returned his glance to her. She was in her late thirties, maybe forty, he guessed, but it was hard to be sure. Her held-in, severe properness could make her seem older than she was, he realized. "I'm Fay Downing. I own the hotel," the woman said.

"Seems a right neat and proper place," Fargo commented.

"And you're thinking it doesn't fit in with the rest of the town," Fay Downing said, and her smile was coolly proper.

"Something like that," Fargo admitted.

"I keep it that way. We eliminate a number of rowdy types by allowing only those guests willing to obey our rules," the woman said with a definite prim authority in her face.

"And I can guess what they are," Fargo said. "No drinking, no gambling, no women in your room unless you're properly man and wife."

Fay Downing's smile was coolly proper again with, he noted, a touch of condescension in it. "I'm sure you'll abide with our rules, Mr. Fargo. Besides, we've had a room ready for you." She smiled again as his brows lifted, and without the cool condescension in it, it was a nice smile, he decided. "General Taylor is a friend of mine. He told me you were expected," she said. "I'm sure you'll enjoy your stay, brief as it may be." She bestowed another smile on him and turned and walked away. The very proper dress couldn't completely hide the slow, sensuous movement of her hips. Some things primness couldn't control.

Fargo took the key from the desk clerk.

"Stable's at the back of the hotel," the man said, and Fargo went outside and led the Ovaro around to the rear of the building to find a small stable almost as neat as the hotel with water buckets all neatly in place, the floor swept clean, and tack hung in a tidy row against the walls. An elderly stableboy emerged to eye the magnificent black-and-white horse with appreciation.

"We'll give him the box stall. Don't get many like that," the man said.

"Much obliged." Fargo nodded and strolled away. He walked to the front of the hotel as night descended, and headed toward the nearest dance hall, which advertised food as well as drink. He had a roast-beef sandwich and a bourbon and found himself thinking about Fay Downing. She was the third female that had known he was on his way here. It seemed that General Taylor was very talkative to the ladies. At least Fay Downing hadn't greeted him with demands and hot lead, and he decided to be grateful for small favors.

He finished his meal, firmly but pleasantly turned away three girls, and sauntered out into the night. He made his way back to the end of town and the Claysville Hotel when he spotted a young woman carrying a cloth sack with laundry overflowing the top of it.

The short light-brown hair bounced as she walked, and her small, trim figure seemed even tighter and trimmer than he'd remembered. She saw him almost as he did her, and a tiny furrow instantly dug into her brow. She walked toward two wagons, one an old

Conestoga, the other an Owensboro Texas wagon out-
fitted with steel bows and a canvas top that turned it
into a closed wagon. "I see you got here," Sally Jamison tossed at him.

"No thanks to you."

"My pa was wrong about you being a good and fair-
minded man," she said accusingly.

"My pa told me to stay away from walleyed horses
and wild-talking women."

"There's wild-talking and there's determined."

"And there's plain dumb," he said, and watched
her turn and put the sack of laundry down against the
front wheel of the old Conestoga. "Seems as though
you've a powerful lot of laundry for one small girl,"
Fargo observed.

He saw her eyes narrow but not before he caught
the moment of surprise that touched her face. "I let it
pile up, not that it's any of your business," Sally said,
and lifted the sack and tossed it into the front opening
of the old Conestoga. Perhaps an honest answer, Fargo
grunted silently, and perhaps not, and he wondered
what else Sally Jamison was holding back besides ex-
planations.

"Nothing's changed," she said coldly. "You remember that, Fargo."

"Nothing," he agreed. "You remember that, too,
honey." She tossed him another glare and disappeared
into the Conestoga, and he walked on to the prim,
carnation-bordered hotel, grimly certain he hadn't seen
the last of Sally Jamison. But he'd taught her one lesson and given her a warning that might make her think
twice about any foolishness, and he settled for the
thought as he entered the hotel and went to his room.
It was on the first floor at the end of a dimly lighted
corridor, and he halted at the door before slipping the
key into the lock, listened, drew in a deep breath,
waited, and finally opened the door. The caution was

part of him, especially when he received the kind of reception he'd encountered this far.

Light from an outside lamp illuminated the room enough for him to see a large, brass bed, a dresser with a white porcelain basin, a water pitcher atop it, and a closet. He undressed, hung his holster over the bedpost within easy reach, and stretched out naked across the top sheet on the bed. He let his thoughts idle and wondered if the striking, raven-haired young woman was also in town someplace. Or had she fled? he grunted. Perhaps General Morton Taylor would have some explanation for the two young women, he pondered.

Fargo had begun to turn onto his side when he heard the knock at the door, a soft, polite knock. He sat up and his hand drew the Colt from the bedpost in one quick, fluid motion. "Come in," he said, and the Colt was aimed at the door, which slowly pushed open just enough to let the tall, narrow figure slip inside the room.

He stared in surprise at Fay Downing and drew the top sheet over his groin. She wore a floor-length brown nightdress of some material that could've been cotton. It buttoned to the top at her neck and hung loosely to almost completely hide her body inside its folds.

"Came for a visit," Fay said, and brushed one hand across the brown hair, still severely pulled back.

"Aren't you violating your own rules, no women in the rooms?" Fargo asked.

"I never said that was one of our rules. You did," Fay Downing said coolly.

"You saying I was wrong?" Fargo smiled.

"Quite wrong," the woman answered. "We have only one rule here, but it does, as I said, eliminate a number of rowdy types."

"What's that?" Fargo inquired.

"Don't disturb the other guests. You can do whatever you like here, but do it quietly."

Fargo let a broad grin slide across his face. "All this prim and proper appearance is something of a mask, then, isn't it?" he commented.

Fay Downing shrugged and took a step closer to him and he watched her eyes move across the beauty of his hard-muscled body, naked except for the portion of sheet he'd pulled across his groin. She halted at the side of the bed, reached one hand up, and pulled a clip from her severely pulled-back hair. The brown locks tumbled down instantly to wreathe her face, and whatever her age was, she looked five years younger, Fargo noted. Her hand went to the top button of the nightdress, pulled it open, and moving quickly, did the same with the others until the dress was half-unbuttoned. She wriggled her shoulders and the dress slid from her and fell in a ring at her feet and she stood absolutely nude before him.

Fargo frowned as he took in her body: narrow hips, breasts no longer held flat and ballooning out with surprising deep curves, a narrow waist, and a very, very black and tangled triangle. Long legs still held firmness and, while not extraordinary, were serviceably attractive. While the surprise stabbed at him, he felt the sheet over his groin begin to lift as he quickly responded to the sight of her and the very unmistakable glow in her eyes.

"We'll talk . . . but later," she said, and slowly lowered herself to the edge of the bed.

"Never argue with the management," Fargo said, and pulled the sheet away. He watched Fay Downing's eyes widen with appreciation as they riveted on his throbbing, standing maleness, and he caught the quick intake of her breath.

"Oh, oh, Jesus," she breathed, and Fay Downing came toward him almost crawling on all fours, to fall against him. She rubbed deep-curved breasts back and forth across him and he felt their softness even as large, brownish-pink nipples rose up from their light-brown

27

areolae. His surprise quickly gave way to desire. Her skin was hot and her hands dug into his shoulders as, her mouth open, she pressed her lips devouringly over his. His hands came up to cup both of the deep breasts and his thumbs rubbed lightly across the firm nipples. Fay Downing made a deep, guttural sound as she raised her legs and brought her long, narrow-hipped body over his. The black, tangly triangle pushed back and forth against his organ and she lifted her torso, brought it down, lifted again, came down once more as she sought to impale herself on the throbbing, pulsing spear.

"I want, Fargo, Jesus, I want," Fay Downing breathed.

"Yes, you do, honey," Fargo agreed. "You sure do."

With his last word she came down over him and her cry was a sudden guttural shriek as she took in all of him, pressed down hard and lifted at once, and came down again with something close to ferocity. "Oh, ah . . . Jeeeesus, aaaagh," Fay Downing gasped out while she pumped furiously atop him and, with each motion, rammed her breasts against his mouth. "Yes, yes, yes, ah, ah, aaaagh," she breathed as she continued to pump her torso up and down on him. He lifted with her increasingly frantic motions, rose up, and thrust back upward, and the woman groaned and her head fell from side to side. "Ah, ah, good, aaah, so good . . . aaaah," Fay Downing murmured, and he suddenly felt her long legs come in tight around him, knees pressing into his hips. "Now, oh, my God, now . . . aaaaggggh," she half-screamed, half-growled, and fell across him.

He found one deep breast in his mouth as she quivered on top of him, holding him throbbingly tight inside her as she made muttered sounds, animallike groans that were drawn from someplace deep inside her. As her narrow-hipped body quivered atop him, he held her, bit gently into the deep-cupped breast, and finally felt her go limp. With another hissing groan she fell from atop him to lay trembling at his side, her mouth open and gasping in air. Her glance slowly focused on his face, took another moment, and then she let a smile edge her lips . . . and Fay Downing was suddenly a most attractive woman, her long, narrow form graceful with young-girl echoes.

"Surprised, aren't you?" she murmured.

"Can't say I'm not," Fargo admitted. "The hotel isn't alone in wearing a prim and proper mask."

She pushed herself up on both elbows and her breasts curved beautifully upward. "Everybody wears masks," she said. "Different reasons, different masks."

"Why'd you come here now?" Fargo asked. "Not just because you're hungry and horny."

She smiled again. "That was part of it," Fay Downing said.

"What's the rest?" Fargo pressed.

"General Taylor," she answered, and Fargo's brows lifted in surprise. "I know he hired you. I want you to stay hired. I want to be sure you'll take him through."

"You know what this is all about?" Fargo questioned.

"No. I told you General Taylor is a friend of mine. He's really more than that. He backed me in this hotel and promised to back me in a series of others if his plans, whatever they are, go through. His success is my success, you could say. That's why I want you to stay with him," Fay said, and her smile came again. "Besides, I don't get many men that look like you stopping by here."

"Who do you get here?" Fargo queried.

"Men who have to be careful. Women who have to be discreet," Fay Downing said.

"What if I back off?" Fargo asked. "Don't take the general's offer?"

Fay Downing's white shoulders lifted in a half-shrug. "I'll be real sorry," she said. "But not about tonight."

Fargo felt the smile move across his face. Fay Downing had her own brand of determined integrity, and he reached out and cupped one breast in his hand. "In that case there's no need to leave yet," he murmured.

"None at all," she agreed, and her mouth was open as she pressed her lips to his, instant, devouring hunger coursing through her. He turned her long, narrow-hipped body to him, brought her onto her back as her hands reached for him. She found his organ and cried out even as she began to stroke and squeeze, finger fondling, and she uttered tiny gasps of pleasure as he grew under her touch. "Oh, yes, yes," she breathed, her head nodding for emphasis, and she half-turned her hips as she pulled him to her. "Please, please," Fay Downing entreated, and her legs rose up and fell open, the most persuasive entreaty of all.

Fargo came to her and slowly slid into her warmth and she cried out with a deep, guttural sound that quickly became a series of low groans, deep paeans of passion that grew only in depth until they erupted with her pushing, pumping fever as she climaxed again.

When she lay beside him, long sighing sounds coming from her, he enjoyed the very individual loveliness that was hers, a woman with a still-firm body that echoed a long-legged filly. Finally she rose, swung long legs over the edge of the bed, and drew on the brown nightdress. She buttoned it demurely and pulled her hair back and secured it with a clip. When she walked to the door, she was her proper self and she paused as she opened the door to blow him a kiss. He laughed and lay back as she disappeared into the hallway. Fay

Downing had been another surprise, by far the most pleasant one. She'd used sex instead of a six-gun, and he much preferred that. But he'd had enough surprises for one day and he rose and locked the door before returning to bed and sleep.

He let himself stay asleep until the morning was half over, reveling in the luxury of a good bed and time to waste. When he woke, he used the porcelain pitcher of water to wash and the towels furnished by the hotel. Downstairs, he found a barber employed by the hotel, and enjoyed a smooth, professional shave.

When Fargo went outside, his eyes automatically flicked to Sally Jamison's wagons and they found only empty space. She had moved away in the night, and he wondered not so much where but why. He walked to the stable and paid the stableboy to give the Ovaro a thorough cleaning and grooming.

Slowly, the Trailsman wandered on through Claysville, found a place where he could get a mug of strong coffee, and continued on through the streets of town. Claysville had a movable population of wagon trains and prospectors, he noted. To the north, the flat plateau stretched far to nudge the edge of the Rocky Mountains and to the west it butted against the Sangre de Cristo range, the long, narrow and harsh mountains that ran down into the New Mexico Territory. It was a land where the large and small wagon trains could go north paralleling the mountains, a land where there was good farming soil and, in the high land, silver and gold, precious gems, and valuable minerals for the mining.

There was also the red man, hunter and hunted, tormentor and tormented. The Utes, the Apache, the Navaho, the Comanche and occasionally the Kiowa, their savagery different only in character, their arrows carrying the same death.

But Claysville was a town that existed more on those who passed through it than on those who stayed, and in that it was little different from so many other towns across the plains and prairies.

Fargo watched a line of Studebaker farm wagons slowly move through town, heavy with sacks of oats, corn, and maize. He then casually strolled on and took note that the sun had begun to slide down the late-afternoon sky. He stopped in at the dance hall, downed a bourbon, and finally made his way back to the stables. He took a fresh shirt and clean pair of Levi's from his saddlebag and returned to the hotel, where he changed, and finally went outside to find Fay Downing there watering the carnations with a sprinkler can. She was coolly polite, her expression entirely composed, as if the night had never occurred.

Fargo smiled inwardly. "How do I find General Taylor's place, Miss Downing?" he asked blandly.

"Take the road north from town till you reach a twisted black oak with a split trunk. Take the right fork there and stay on it. You'll come to the general's place. It's surrounded by a circle of gambel oak," she told him.

"Much obliged," he said, swinging onto the Ovaro, and the first purple gray of dusk sifted down as he rode from town. He held the horse at a canter, followed Fay Downing's directions, and came upon the circle of gambel oak about two miles later. The ranchhouse that sat in the center of the circle was long and low, a stone foundation with good hickory over it. The circle of cleared land in front of it was filled with carriages, mostly buckboards, but he spotted a yellow canopy-top surrey and two curtain-quarter rockaways, one green, the other dark red.

Fargo tethered the Ovaro to the hitching post outside the ranch house and walked through the open front door, following the sounds of laughter and conversation, to find himself in the doorway of a huge living room hung with tapestries and crowded with men and women. The men were mostly in their best frock coats

32

and many of the women in evening dress. He waited as an Oriental man in a butler's outfit came toward him. "Tell General Taylor that Skye Fargo's here," the Trailsman said, and the butler disappeared back into the crowd.

Moments later, Fargo watched a big, gray-haired man in a black frock coat and a bright-red cravat push his way through the crowd of partygoers toward him. "Glad you made it, Fargo," the man said, and thrust out a strong, thick-fingered hand. "General Morton Taylor, here." Fargo took in a wide face, a strong jaw and sharp blue eyes, a face accustomed to giving orders. "Come on in and let me introduce you to some of the people who are backing this venture of mine," General Taylor boomed, and Fargo followed his thick-set figure through the crowd. The general halted beside a silver-haired, tall, thin man with an austere, patrician face that seemed as though it belonged to a saint. "Francis Coldstone," the general introduced. The man nodded with austere politeness. "This is the Trailsman, the man who's going to find me a way through," General Taylor said.

"Good. Very good, indeed." Coldstone nodded again, and the general moved on, beckoning Fargo to follow him. He halted and gestured toward a portly man and an equally portly woman beside a table of sandwiches and liquor bottles. "Tom and Harriet Thurston—they're people who know an opportunity when they see one," the general said, and moved on to halt again and nod toward another man busily talking to two ladies in long gowns. "Edmund Alston, another loyal friend and backer," the general murmured. "A fine businessman."

"This is all mighty nice, but there are some things I'd like knowing more about," Fargo said.

"Yes, yes, of course. That's certainly understandable," General Taylor agreed. "We can talk in here." He led the way into an adjoining room that turned out to be a quiet, book-lined study. Fargo waited as the general closed the door behind him and leaned against a cherry-wood desk to face him with an expansive smile. "You ask and I'll answer," the man said.

"Your letter said you wanted me to break trail for you. I've come to wonder what for and where?" Fargo said.

"From here down into New Mexico Territory, just west of Cimarron," General Taylor said. "But I want to stay away from the open plains routes. I want to go down through the Sangre de Cristo Mountains."

Fargo let his lips purse as he frowned. "That's doing it the hard way. If you can get through the mountains, there's the Apache. They all roam those mountains—the Chiricahua, the White Mountain, the Mescalero—and none of them is what you could call friendly."

"I'm aware it will be difficult and dangerous. That's why I sent for you," the general said with an edge of chiding tolerance in his voice.

"What kind of wagon train am I going to be taking through the mountains?" Fargo questioned, his eyes searching the man's wide face.

"Four wagons of oil shale," General Taylor said, and Fargo felt his brows lift.

"Oil shale?"

"Exactly," the general said. "We believe there's a tremendous market for oil shale in New Mexico Territory and we've perfected a process to extract the oil from the shale."

"Why all the secrecy? Why not take the open plains south?"

"There are people in high and low places that want to take over an idea such as this. They'll do anything to stop me. It's vital that I move into New Mexico unobserved," Taylor answered.

Fargo let the reply turn inside his head. He had nothing to tell him the answer wasn't honest, yet he had difficulty in swallowing it whole. "Still seems like a powerful lot of risk for some oil shale," he commented.

"It's worth it, believe me," the general said, and Fargo held the reservations inside himself. "All you have to do is get my wagons through. I've offered you four times the usual fee to do that."

"You have."

"Then that's all that need concern you, Fargo," the general said firmly.

"Can't spend money without your scalp," Fargo said. "How many men are you taking?"

"Ten," the general said, and Fargo's brows lifted again. "More than that would attract too much attention. But they're all excellent shots. We'll actually have more firepower than the average large wagon train. I'll have you meet my foreman, Burt Roscoe, tomorrow. Any other questions?"

Fargo paused for a moment. "How do you come by the 'General'?"

The man smiled proudly. "I was with Sam Houston in Texas. I held the rank of general in his army," he said. "Titles stick with a man."

"Guess so." Fargo nodded

General Taylor pushed away from the desk. "I must be getting back to my guests. We can talk more tomorrow," he said, and pulled the door open. The rush of conversation and murmured noise was instant, and Fargo followed the man from the study.

"Father, there you are. I've been looking for you," Fargo heard the voice call, and he turned to take in the young woman that moved through the crowd toward the general. His gaze caught on the long, free-flowing black hair, the black eyes, and the aquiline nose. No yellow shirt and black riding britches now but an off-the-shoulder gown of delicate pink that made her raven-locked loveliness even more striking.

"I'll be damned," he murmured under his breath,

and saw his own surprise mirrored in the shock in her eyes.

"Sorry, my dear. I had to duck out for a moment," the general said. "This is Skye Fargo, the Trailsman." The young woman blinked, pushed the astonishment from her eyes, and nodded politely. "My daughter, Alanna," the general said to Fargo, and the young woman nodded with a thin smile. But she had been quick to regain her composure, Fargo noted with reluctant admiration. "Alanna, get Mr. Fargo a drink while I see to my other guests," the general said, and moved on amid the other merrymakers.

Fargo's gaze held on the young woman's black eyes, only harshness in his stare. "Bourbon," he slid at her, and she turned and started for the table with the liquor on it. He followed closely and admired the squareness of her bare shoulders, the dress revealing nice shoulder blades and the upper part of a firm back. She halted at the table, poured a shot glass of bourbon, and handed it to him with her eyes narrowed.

"General Morton Taylor's daughter," Fargo murmured. "The world's full of surprises."

"I didn't know he'd asked you here," she said.

"Alanna, honey, you've some answering to do," Fargo said. "Or do I just tell Daddy what you tried to do?"

"No," she said quickly, but there was no panic in her eyes. She kept a firm grip on herself, he noted. "We must talk, I know that," she said.

"You're goddamn right, honey," Fargo growled.

"But not here. I can't talk here," Alanna said. "Tomorrow, noon, at Catfish Pond."

"Where's that?"

"Go straight north from here, over the first hill and past a long line of box elders," Alanna said. "I'll be there, waiting. We'll talk then."

"You don't show and I have a talk with Daddy about his little girl," Fargo warned, and she nodded, her lovely face set tight. He downed the bourbon and strode away from her, found General Taylor playing host, and took him aside. "I'll be back tomorrow afternoon," Fargo said.

"I'll have half your fee waiting for you as promised," the man said.

Fargo nodded agreement and pushed his way through the crowded room to the door. He paused, his eyes scanning the handsomely attired men and women, and he found Alanna, radiantly lovely in the delicate pink gown, and saw her eyes were on him. He held her gaze with a hard stare for another moment and then walked from the house.

His jaw was tight as he swung onto the Ovaro outside, and he found himself thinking about Alanna Taylor. She had been taken as much by surprise as he, but she'd made an instant recovery. She was a very contained, coolly poised young woman, he acknowledged. But she had surprised him twice. He'd make sure she didn't do it a third time.

He pulled the Ovaro to a halt in a dense thicket of the gambel oaks that surrounded the house. He dismounted and settled down against a tree trunk that let him have a clear view of the house. He'd have a long wait, he knew, and he allowed himself to catnap as the hours slowly rolled on.

The sound of the first buckboard rolling away from the house snapped him awake and he saw three others beginning to move. Next came one of the two curtain-quarter rockaways with four people inside it. The other guests began to drift out and climb into their wagons with quickening frequency, and Fargo shifted his position to sit up straighter. He glimpsed the general and caught the glimmer of Alanna's delicate pink gown in the light from the doorway, and when the last buckboard rolled away from the house, he rose to his haunches, his eyes narrowing as he peered through the night. The waiting wasn't over, he realized, and he watched the lights go off inside the house in slow progression. The last to be turned off were those at the far end where, he guessed, the kitchen was quartered.

He bided his time, silent and almost certain it would not be for nothing. Alanna Taylor had been too determined to do him in at their first meeting and too quickly agreeable to talk at this one. But he had decided to go along with the job. And he'd be very careful until all the pieces fit correctly into place.

That thought had just curled in his mind when he saw the figure hurrying from a side door of the house, slender, clad in a black shirt and black britches, raven locks flowing back from her face. She ran on quick, light-footed steps to a barn, and Fargo watched her go inside and, a few moments later, come out leading a brown horse with a white blaze. She walked the horse carefully until she'd reached the edge of the oaks before she mounted and sent the animal into a fast canter.

Fargo climbed onto the Ovaro, let Alanna go by, and fell in behind her. He stayed to the right of the girl as she took the horse north and then west over low hills, riding hard, totally unaware she was being followed. She took a sharp turn at the bottom of a small gulley; he stayed on her tail but was careful to hang back far enough so that she could hear only the sound of her own horse's hoofbeats. He slowed as the little shack came into sight in a small hollow, bordered by a rock formation at the rear and dense foilage on the other three sides.

Fargo pulled the Ovaro to a halt and slid from the saddle as Alanna Taylor reined up in front of the shack. He crept closer on foot after leading the Ovaro into the trees and dropped to one knee as the door of the shack opened and a man came out. He wore boots, trousers, and his gun belt, and a three-quarter moon lighted a sharp face with hard lines, a thin mouth, and eyes that glinted even in the half-light.

"What in hell you doin' here at this hour?" the man rasped at Alanna Taylor.

"Got a special job for you, Krawfell," the girl said. "And I want this one done properly. I hope you'll do better than those last three misfits you sent me."

"I'm listenin'," the man muttered.

"I'm meeting Fargo at noon tomorrow, at Catfish Pond. I want you there and I want it to go right this time. He's not to be killed. I want him shot in the leg so he won't be able to ride. That'll be enough to stop him from taking the wagons out. That's all I want, do you understand?"

The man shrugged but his face didn't change its cold expression. "He shoots at me. I shoot back. I can't promise a shot won't go wrong."

"You shoot first and carefully and nothing can go wrong," Alanna answered.

The man shrugged as he answered. "I get paid first, like before," he said.

Fargo saw Alanna hesitate, then dig a hand into the pocket of her trousers and give Krawfell a roll of bills. "I'll expect you to follow instructions," she said, and pulled herself onto her horse. She rode quickly away and Fargo stayed in place as she disappeared from sight, then he brought his eyes back to the figure standing outside the shack.

"I don't take chances, bitch," he heard the man growl.

As Krawfell went back into the cabin, a hard smile edged Fargo's lips. The man was a hired gunslinger. He not only wouldn't take chances, he wouldn't even try to follow her orders. Slowly, Fargo pulled himself to his feet and led the Ovaro out of the trees, climbed onto the horse, and turned north. He wasn't about to take chances, either.

3

The early-morning sun came in on a cool breeze. Fargo found the long line of boxelders and the small, oblong-shaped pond at the end of it. He'd bedded down for the remainder of the night and took to the saddle with the first dawn rays and now he slowly circled the pond that sparkled with clear blue water under the new sun. Trees, mostly black oak and boxelder, grew close to the water's edge for the most part, and when he completed circling the pond, he dismounted and led the Ovaro into the thick trees near the front end, where the pond narrowed. The land rose and he halted at a place that let him look down at the water and offered a narrow pathway up across a low rise to the rear.

He settled down to wait and listened to the songs of the meadowlarks that congregated near the pond. The sun was still at least an hour away from the noon sky when he spotted the lone horseman slowly approach the pond. The rider drew closer and halted almost at the water's edge and Fargo watched the man's eyes scan the brush and trees that grew close to the shoreline. In the daylight, the hired gunslinger's face was a hard mask, his thin mouth a tight-lipped line that turned down at the corners. Krawfell continued to scan the brush and trees and Fargo watched him slowly move his horse away from the edge of the pond and into a place where two black oaks bent toward each other to form a leafy curtain. The Trailsman peered down and watched the brush move as Krawfell disappeared from sight in the trees. The brush moved again, more vigorously this time, as Krawfell turned his horse inside the foliage and then, in a few moments more, stopped moving entirely.

Fargo's lake-blue eyes were hard as he carefully peered at the place where Krawfell had hidden himself. Skye measured distances, angles, gauged the chances as best he could, and finally led the Ovaro back up across the low rise and down the other side. He didn't mount the horse until he was far down the slope and then he made a wide circle. When the sun reached the noon sky, he once again rode toward Catfish Pond from the front. He took his time and saw Alanna waiting near the water's edge, standing a few paces from her horse. He flicked a glance toward the two oaks from under his eyelids, moved the Ovaro to the left, and dismounted to put Alanna between himself and the place where Krawfell lay in wait.

She wore a white, man's shirt and black riding skirt. He caught her nervousness in the way her hands clenched the riding crop she held. "Talk," Fargo bit out, and saw Alanna Taylor's lips tighten.

"I suppose you want to know why I'm trying to stop my father from going on this trip," she said. He kept the smile inside himself. She was stalling for time.

"No, I just came to get your ideas on riding side-saddle."

"There's no need to be sarcastic," Alanna said, but he saw her lips twitch nervously.

Krawfell would only wait for a few moments, Fargo knew, then he'd try to hit his target even with Alanna in the way. The gunslinger wasn't the kind to be patient, and it was vital he didn't get the first shot in. He had to be delayed another few moments. Fargo moved, casually, and began to place himself on the other side of Alanna. Krawfell would hold his fire, now, waiting for his target to move into the perfect position. Shooting a man in the back was always safest.

41

"I'm still listening," Fargo said to Alanna, and now she couldn't hide the nervousness in her eyes. He took another half-step to his right and put his back squarely to the two oak trees. But as he did, with but a split second gone by, he whirled as he dropped into a crouch. He had the Colt in his hand, firing furiously, and he emptied the gun into the thick brush between the two oaks.

The gasped groan rose before he'd finished firing and Krawfell tumbled forward into the open, his body spouting red in at least three places as he lay face down and lifeless. Fargo straightened up, turned to Alanna, and saw her lovely face wreathed in horror as she stared down at the gunslinger. "You knew . . . you knew he was hiding there," she gasped.

"I did," Fargo agreed as he reloaded the Colt. "And I knew he wasn't going to shoot me in the leg. He wasn't the kind to take a chance that I'd turn and put a bullet through him."

The girl's black eyes grew round with surprise. "You know what I said to him," she breathed. "Then you know I didn't want you killed."

"I know," Fargo said, and his hand shot out with the speed of a rattler's strike. He closed one fist around her shirt front and yanked her to him. "And that's the only reason I don't take your hide off, honey," he growled. "Which I still might do unless I get some straight answers from you."

He let go of her and she stepped back and pushed aside the moment of fear. She drew a deep breath and the white shirt tightened around the long curve of her breasts. "I've tried every way I know to stop my father from this and he won't listen to me."

"Why? You've something against this oil-shale venture?"

Alanna Taylor's lovely lips drew back in disdain. "There's no oil-shale venture. That story's a complete lie. It's all a front for the real thing."

42

"Which is?"

"He's going down to make New Mexico an independent republic, just as Sam Houston did with the Republic of Texas. It's been an obsession with him ever since he was with Houston. Only Daddy says he knows what went wrong in Texas and he won't make the same mistakes."

"You don't believe that."

"No, I don't. He'll be killed. The United States government knows something is going on. They're waiting to catch him at something and put him in prison. The Mexicans are against it. They're afraid it'll upset the results of the treaty of Guadalupe-Hildalgo and the monies still going to them. They'll kill him if they can."

"He's got to be aware of all that," Fargo said.

"He's convinced he can win in spite of everything. He has an organized group in New Mexico waiting to take over. Now that his rich friends are backing him, he's ready to move. But they're only putting up money. It's his life on the line and I don't want to see him killed or imprisoned. He's a stubborn man but he's my father and I love him."

"And you want to save him from himself."

"Yes. Now maybe you can understand."

"Doesn't change anything for me. I've been hired to do a job and I'm going to do it," he said. "And I'd best not get any more trouble from you, honey."

"Your job means more to you than anything else, I see," she flung at him, her black eyes flashing.

"Wild talk doesn't mean much, that's for sure."

"It's not wild talk."

"So you say. But your story doesn't hang right. He wouldn't need a front of this oil-shale shipment to go down and set his coup into operation. He could just go down and start things moving."

Alanna frowned and bit her lips. "Yes, I thought of

43

that, too. There has to be a reason for all this disguise. But that doesn't mean you can't believe me, dammit.''

''Doesn't mean I can, either. You could be having a private war with your pa, maybe for years. Maybe you figure his money ought to stay safe so it'll be yours someday and not go into some wild scheme. Or maybe you're just a plain, spoiled little bitch who wants everything her way.''

''You are a bastard,'' Alanna blazed.

Fargo laughed as he swung onto the Ovaro. ''Flattery will get you nowhere, honey,'' he said. ''Let's go.''

She climbed onto her horse with her lips tight. ''Where are you going?''

''To your pa's place. We can ride together. That'll be real cozy,'' Fargo said, and drew a quick glare.

''You'll find out I've told you the truth about everything,'' Alanna pronounced. ''You remember that.''

''I don't want any more trouble out of you. You remember that,'' Fargo returned, his voice growing hard.

''You don't have to worry about that. I've nothing left now,'' she said. ''I'm just going to try and keep my father alive.''

''What's that mean exactly?''

''It means I'm going along,'' she said. ''Maybe I can still convince him to give this whole mad idea up.''

''Your pa, your neck. Does he know you're going?'' Fargo said.

''Yes,'' she said quietly. ''But that's all he knows, of course.'' She shot a sideways glance at the big man riding beside her. ''I'd be grateful if you'd keep it that way.''

''That depends on you, sweetie,'' Fargo answered, and she took the reply in silence.

The circle of gambel oaks and the big ranch house came into view, and Alanna remained silent. Fargo pondered everything she had told him and knew he didn't entirely disbelieve her. Her story made some of the pieces fit better than they had, but the main one still didn't take it's place. Why the oil-shale front just to go into New Mexico to start a coup? It still seemed unnecessary, and even Alanna had no answer for it. He turned off his thoughts as they rode to the house and Morton Taylor emerged.

"We met on the road," Alanna sang out cheerily. "Had a nice talk." She hopped to the ground and planted a big kiss on her father's cheek. "See you all later," she said as she hurried into the house.

Fargo watched her go, hips swinging smoothly. She could carry things well, he noted, and he took a moment to wonder if she were still going to play games with him or if she'd learned better.

"Come around to the rear of the house," General Taylor said.

Fargo slid from the saddle and followed him to where he saw the four wagons lined up, a number of men lounging beside them. Owensboro platform spring drays, Fargo noted, cut-under wheels with chains from axle to doubletree, easily able to carry their heavy load of shale. Strong, yet able to negotiate sharp turns, Fargo grunted silently. The general had chosen well.

"Got hold of four good teams, Morgans mixed with Cleveland bays," Morton Taylor said. "Powerful but not too heavy-footed." He motioned and one of the men detached himself from the others and approached. Fargo saw a medium-height man, a weathered face with cool blue eyes, a sturdy, no-nonsense type, the kind of man who did his job well but without imagination. "My foreman, Burt Roscoe," the general introduced. "Burt will be in charge of the men. He's picked each one himself."

Fargo let his glance go past Burt Roscoe to the nine men beside the wagons. No youngsters, he noted, all hardened hands, a few a little too grim-faced for his liking, one very tall with hostility in his eyes. But they'd all work hard and fight well, he was certain and returned his gaze to the foreman. "My men will be riding herd on the wagons every minute we move. You want something different, you tell me,'' Burt Roscoe said.

"If and when," Fargo agreed, and followed the general back to the house. "Still makes only twelve men, counting you," he said.

"But good men, hard men. They'll make more firepower than a ten-wagon train can mount," the general said.

"And Alanna," Fargo remarked, and saw the man's face stiffen. "Why is she coming along?"

"Because she's of age. She can do whatever she wants," the general said. "And I'd like her to see my success for herself."

"What success is that?" Fargo said.

"Why, that of this venture," the general replied with a touch of defensiveness. "She hasn't any real faith in it. I want her to see she's been wrong."

Fargo nodded but the answer had told him nothing. "Still seems you're taking an awful big risk for this thing."

"It will be worth it," the general said. "And it's necessary." Fargo cast an eye at the fast-fading afternoon light and strolled to the Ovaro. "We're ready to leave, come morning," General Taylor said, reached into his pocket, and handed Fargo a roll of bills.

"I'll be here," Fargo said, nodding to the man.

He rode slowly back toward Claysville and thought about the very different stories he'd been told about the general's pilgrimage into the New Mexico Territory. Neither held together properly but he kept thinking that Alanna had concocted her story in hopes it'd turn him away. It just didn't make sense to take four wagons into Apache mountains as a cover, not when there were a dozen easier ways for the general to go into New Mexico. He had to go along with the general's explanation for now, Fargo decided, and he turned west and explored the flat prairie land. He found three long flat gulleys that dipped below the line of the plains but saw that for the most part the wagons would travel through wide open flatland for a good distance before reaching the foothills of the Sangre de Cristo range.

The dusk gave way to night and he turned back, again heading slowly for Claysville. He got something to eat at one of the dance halls, downed the food with a bourbon, and casually returned to the neat hotel.

"I'll take that room again for the night," he said to the desk clerk.

"Miss Downing had it held for you," the man said.

"Miss Downing's real thoughtful." Fargo smiled and took the key the man held out to him.

"There was a young lady asking for you," the clerk said. "Didn't leave a name."

"Smallish girl, short light-brown hair and a little nose?" Fargo inquired.

"That's the one." The clerk nodded. "Didn't leave a message, either. Just wanted to know what room you were in."

Fargo let his lips purse as he started down the corridor toward the room. Only one small wall lamp burned at the far end and the hallway was mostly a dark and shadowy place. If Sally Jamison had come snooping, there was a reason. He halted at the closed door of the room, leaned forward, and let his nostrils take in deep drafts of air. He caught it on the third try, the faint scent of powder and cologne, and a thin smile traced itself across his face. It was probably easy enough to slip past the old desk clerk, he reasoned. Or she might have come in through the window, which was certainly low enough to the ground. But she was inside, waiting, and his hand was on the butt of the Colt as he entered the room.

The outside lamplight was enough to let him take in the room at a quick glance. It was empty but the scent of powder grew stronger, and as he crossed to the bed, he saw that the door to the closet hung open, just a fraction but enough for someone inside to peer into the room through the narrow space. He sat down on the bed, unstrapped the gun belt, and set it down beside him. Slowly, he took off his clothes until he was naked, and he rose, stretched his powerful, beautifully balanced body, went to the window for a moment, and then sat back on the bed. This time he used the headboard to rest against in a sitting position and he slowly drew a corner of the sheet over his maleness. He kept the Colt at his side but flat on the bedsheet.

"You can come out now, Sally Jamison. Show's over," he said calmly. He waited, and after a long moment, the closet door swung open and he watched her step into the room. She wore dark Levi's and a dark-green shirt, and in one hand she held a pistol, an old Colt Navy model belt pistol, a single-action piece with rounded trigger and a loading lever. "What were you going to do with that?" he asked chidingly.

"Make you listen to me, or else," she glowered.

"You're a slow learner, aren't you?" Fargo said. "And I see you took the time to watch."

"I couldn't help that," she said, and he saw the color come into her cheeks. "I had to wait till you were relaxed."

"Steer shit, sweetie." Fargo grinned cheerfully. "You could've come out anytime. Now put that damn gun down before I get up and fan your little ass."

Her glower returned and she held the pistol without moving. "Not until you promise to listen to me."

"I always listen. Start by telling me why you have to go along with the general's wagons?" Fargo said.

"It's the only way I can get to look for my folks," she said, and Fargo frowned in surprise but surprise was getting to be pretty damn common on this job, he reminded himself. "They went into the Sangre de Cristo range almost a year ago to prospect for gold and gems. They never came back and I want to find out why. But I can't go alone. That'd be suicide."

"It would," Fargo agreed.

48

"But going along with another wagon train, especially one as well-guarded as General Taylor's, would let me do it. I could try to find out what happened to my folks. It's my only chance. That's why I have to go along with his wagons," Sally said.

Fargo's eyes held on Sally Jamison as he turned her words in his mind. "Why'd you move your wagons last night?" he slid at her, and saw the flash of surprise touch her face.

"I didn't like where they were," she said. "Too near the road."

"Why do you need two wagons?"

"One for supplies and one in case my folks should be hurt or sick," she answered.

Too quickly, he grunted to himself, a prepared answer. Yet her reasons could be real enough, he mused. She was certainly desperately determined and he'd take her story on the face of it. For now, he added silently. "I'll ask the general. I'll do that for you."

"No, don't ask him. He might say no. Tell him I go along or you won't break trail for him."

"Damn, you've not lost any of your brass, have you? I won't tell him any damn thing like that, honey. I'm going to break trail for the man whether he tells you to come along, get lost, or go to hell."

"Then you don't go," she said, raising the pistol.

"How's that going to help you find out about your folks?" Fargo tossed at her.

"I told you: you don't go, he doesn't go. He'll have to find somebody else. Maybe they'll be more willing to help me," Sally Jamison said.

"Maybe they won't," Fargo answered.

"I'll have to take that chance. At least I'll have another try at it. This way you all just go off without me," she returned. "Dammit, Fargo, all you have to do is tell him to take me along."

Fargo seemed to consider her reply as he measured the distance to the pistol. He needed to distract her for

49

a split second, he decided. "Maybe I could," he said thoughtfully, and pulled the sheet from his groin. Her eyes went to his nakedness, held there for a fascinated moment, and it was all the time he needed. "But I'm not," he bit out as he dived foreward, his hand closing around the barrel of the pistol and twisting it from her hand.

"Damn you," she spit out as she tried to grab for the pistol, but he swung one arm and caught her across the back and she flew face down onto the bed. He was straddling her instantly and held her head down against the bed with one hand. He felt the warmth of her round, tight little rear as he sat atop her.

"I warned you not to point a gun at me again, honey," he growled. "Just for this I wouldn't ask the general the time of day for you." He let his hand go from the back of her neck and swung himself off her rear. "Now, you get your ass out of here, Sally Jamison," he growled, emptied the pistol, and tossed it onto the bed beside her.

"Not till you put something on," she said.

"A sudden attack of principles?" Fargo snapped. "Looking didn't bother you in the closet." She made no reply and stayed facedown across the bed. "Or don't you trust yourself?" Fargo asked. Again she said nothing and remained motionless and he reached for his Levi's and began to draw them on. "All right, it's worth it just to get you the hell out of here," he grumbled.

She turned, finally, when he had the Levi's on, and she pushed herself from the bed and he saw her amber eyes blink and her face grow almost contrite. "Please, Fargo, ask him," she said. "Try to convince him to take me along."

Damn, he swore under his breath. She was the damnedest mixture of contradictions; gun-toting hellion, demanding little bitch, ruthlessly determined daughter, and now a plaintive, appealing supplicant, waiflike and contrite. "Please, Fargo," she said, took a step forward, and her hand came up to press against his chest. "You can make him listen to you."

"I told you I'll ask, nothing more," he said. "Where do I find you, come morning?"

"Here, outside the hotel," Sally said. "I'll be real beholden to you." She drew the warm touch of her hand away and he grimaced at her.

"How'd you come in?" he asked, and she nodded to the window. "Leave the same way," he growled.

She obeyed at once and he watched her climb out of the window and disappear outside. He drew a deep sigh, almost of relief. He wasn't completely sure he'd be having a return visit from Fay Downing, but he didn't want company if it happened. He pulled off trousers and stretched out on the bed. But Sally Jamison was still a question mark. Everything involved in this job was a question mark, he corrected himself. His thoughts continued to idle when the soft knock interrupted and he sat up, waited, and watched the door open. Fay Downing slipped into the room and this time her hair wasn't pulled back severely but hung loose around her face and the high-buttoned, proper dress had been replaced by a light-blue cotton robe.

"Change your style, Miss Downing?" Fargo smiled? "No more masks?"

"No, but sometimes convenience is more important than appearance." She had pulled the robe open by the time she reached the bed. Completely nude underneath, she folded the long, narrow-hipped body against him and once again throbbed with hunger as her mouth closed upon his. No girlish coyness with Fay Downing, only womanly desire, and he met her eagerness with his own surging response.

When her guttural cry finally spiraled from the walls of the room, she fell alongside him, her long, white, narrow-hipped body drawing in deep breaths. She had come wanting, given every part of her in pleasure, and now lay thoroughly satisfied beside him. She rose on one elbow after a spell and regarded him with faint amusement.

"You met with the general, I assume," she said.

"I did. Met Alanna, too," Fargo said. "What do you know about her?" He made the question sound more casual than it was, and Fay Downing shrugged.

"Headstrong. Wants everything her way. She'd like Daddy to stop his ventures and stay home. But she loves him very much. She's fierce in protecting him and I give her credit for that," the woman said, and Fargo grimaced inwardly. Her answer had both hit at and supported Alanna's story and left him no further than he'd been.

"What about Fay Downing?" Fargo asked. "What does she know about this oil-shale venture?"

"Only that the general told me he's going to come back rich and famous and I should be ready to open a chain of hotels."

Fargo nodded. It'd take the journey itself to sort out truth from fancy tales, he decided, and he watched as Fay Downing rose, her long frame curving inward at the waist, and she suddenly looked tired.

"Take care of him, Fargo," she said.

"That self-interest or something more?" Fargo asked.

"Both," she said. "Surprised?"

"Nothing around here surprises me anymore," Fargo commented, and Fay Downing slipped into her robe, blew him a kiss, and left the room without another word. He lay back on the bed, refused to play with the idle thoughts that skipped through his mind, and drew sleep around himself. The morning would come quickly enough, he knew.

4

When Fargo rode into the general's ranch, he saw the men just starting to pull heavy tarpaulin covers over the shale in each wagon.

"The tarps will let us make better time without losing cargo," the general said as Fargo came to a halt. "You're early, Fargo."

"Got a question for you, General," Fargo said. "Met this gal who keeps hounding me about joining up with your wagons."

"That damn Jamison girl?" The man frowned. "Hell, I told her no twice. First time I caught her snooping around the wagons, second time when she stopped me in Claysville with some story about her folks."

Fargo swore silently but he'd decided on his approach and he'd carry it through. "More wagons might be a good thing. Could make Indians decide against an attack," he tried.

"No, absolutely not. No outside wagons near mine," the general barked, and Fargo felt surprise at the sudden harshness in his voice. "We'll be ready to leave within the hour."

"I'll be here," Fargo said, turned the Ovaro in a circle, and put the horse into a fast canter.

Sally Jamison leaned on the fence outside the Claysville hotel when he reined to a halt, her wagons still out of view. A white shirt too big for her and hanging loose over a black riding skirt made her appear smaller and more helpless than she was.

"Dammit, you didn't tell me you'd already asked him," Fargo threw at her, and swung to the ground.

"You didn't ask me," Sally said airily.

"I felt like a damn fool," Fargo snapped.

She stepped closer to him, her light-brown eyes wide. "He turned you down," she murmured, and he nodded. "That was all of it?" she probed.

"I asked. I told you that was all I'd do," Fargo said, and watched her carefully. But she only shrugged, put a hand against his chest and brushed his cheek with a quick touch of her lips.

"I shouldn't have asked more. Thanks for trying," said Sally Jamison, and stepped back. Fargo felt the frown creasing his brow. She'd taken him aback. He'd expected more demands and threats. She was as changeable as a summer wind, he decided.

"There'll be somebody else come along," he said to her as he started to remount.

"No, there won't. But don't you fret about me," she said, and the frown stayed on the big man's face. The turnabout was out of character. Or was it? He pondered. He didn't really know her at all. Maybe the rest had been all bluff and bluster.

"Good luck," he tossed back at her as he rode away, and she nodded gravely and stayed in front of the hotel. He put the Ovaro into a trot, anxious to leave Sally Jamison and her changeable ways behind him.

When he reached the general's place, he saw that the four wagons were tightly covered with their tarpaulins and drew a nod from Burt Roscoe. General Taylor emerged from the house with Alanna and Fargo saw she wore the yellow shirt that heightened the striking effect of her black locks. He let his glance survey the scene of four wagons and three packhorses. The general pulled himself onto a heavy-rumped dapple-gray and Alanna had her brown mare with the white face.

"I spotted a few gulleys we can take that'll keep you off the open plains for a little while," Fargo said.

"Anything helps," General Taylor said, half-turned in the saddle, raised one arm in a wave, and the four heavy drays started to roll.

One driver per wagon left six men riding guard, Fargo noted. Burt Roscoe had put two at the rear of the last wagon, the other four strung out alongside the train.

Fargo had swung to the front of the line when he looked back and saw a small cloud of dust fast approaching, and he frowned as two wagons took shape, with Sally driving the first one, the second tied onto the tailgate of the first.

"What the hell's she doing here?" he heard the general roar. "I told you to tell her no."

"I did," Fargo said as he silently swore at Sally Jamison.

"Well, we'll tell her again, the hard way," the general snapped, and spurred the dapple-gray toward the wagons.

Sally had the Conestoga in the lead, Fargo saw, and she slowed to a walk about a hundred yards back. He sent the Ovaro after the general and was alongside the man as he reined to a halt.

"You're not joining up with my wagons, dammit," the general roared. "You try and I'll put a load of buckshot up your sassy ass and chop your wagons into little pieces."

Fargo watched Sally regard him with a cool but unfazed stare. "I'm not joining your old wagon train," she said. "But it's a free country. I can go wherever I choose to go."

"What's that mean?" General Taylor frowned.

"It means if I want to follow along the trail your wagons have smoothed, I can do so. I can go up the

55

mountains and down the mountains behind you. I can go wherever I please," she said, and Fargo shook his head in a kind of grim admiration. The general threw a frown his way and Fargo shrugged.

"I'm afraid she's right," he said.

"Goddammit, I don't want anybody tailing behind me," the general said.

Sally's voice answered, more sharpness in it. "You can go behind me. I don't care," she said. "But it's a free country and I'll go wherever I want to go whether you like it or not."

Fargo saw the man's face harden. "You could outsmart yourself, young woman," he warned.

"I'll worry about that when the time comes," Sally returned.

"Just see that you stay back, you understand?" Taylor roared.

"Perfectly," Sally said calmly, and the general spurred his horse into a gallop.

Fargo frowned at Sally's smug expression. "He could be right, you know. You could outsmart yourself," he said. "I don't know the man well enough. I don't know to what lengths he'd go."

"I'm sure you won't let him do anything wrong," Sally said with her eyes round.

"Goddamn," Fargo sputtered as he sent the Ovaro galloping away. She knew how to pull every string in her bow, he frowned, and he caught up to the general at the front of the four drays.

"I'll see that we lose her somewhere along the way," the general growled. "I'm not taking company along behind me."

"She may just drop away. It'll be a lot harder than she realizes," Fargo said even though he knew it'd take some catastrophy to make Sally Jamison drop away. "You just keep heading west for now. I'm going to ride on ahead. I'll be waiting for you somewhere."

He started the Ovaro forward and slowed as Alanna pulled alongside.

"I'll ride along," she said.

"If you don't get in the way and follow orders," Fargo grunted.

"I'll try," Alanna said, a note of condescension in her voice, and he set off at a trot. She stayed with him and he enjoyed the way her longish breasts swayed from side to side as she rode, pushing little points into the yellow shirt as they did. "That girl anything special to you?" Alanna asked casually.

"No more than you," Fargo answered.

"What's that mean?"

"Every woman's special in her own way, some are specially good, some specially bad, some specially nice, some specially rotten."

"Just like men."

"But different," Fargo returned. "The goodness is different and the badness is different."

"Philosophical opinions?"

"Experience," Fargo said, and reined to a halt at the mouth of the first gulley. "We can get some water up ahead."

"How do you know?" Alanna asked.

He pointed to a stretched-out flight of doves that swooped low to the ground a half-mile on. "Birds fly to water in the morning, away from it in the evening," he said. "We'll wait here for the others to catch up to us."

Alanna dismounted with a nice, easy motion and regarded Fargo with a slightly bemused glance. "You didn't believe anything I told you, did you?" she asked.

"Sorry." He shrugged.

"Because of all this oil-shale disguise."

"That's right. You can't even explain that," Fargo said. "There's no reason for it."

57

"I can't, but I'm right," she snapped. "What are you going to do when you find out I'm right?"

"Can't say. I don't like to be sold a bill of goods, but if nobody's the worse for it, I'll live with it."

"Don't you care that what he wants to do is all wrong? It can't work, any more than it did for Sam Houston."

"A man's got the right to make his own mistakes," Fargo said, and drew a hiss of disagreement from her. He squatted down to the ground, letting his eyes sweep the soil in the gulley.

"What do you see?" Alanna asked.

"Animal tracks, mostly. Deer, raccoon, possum, jackrabbits."

"Meaningless," she remarked.

"Nothing's meaningless. Animal tracks can tell you a lot."

"Such as?"

"What kind of vegetation is near, if something scared them into running, how much game is available for supper, and sometimes they mark trails, especially antelope and deer," he said.

She broke off another question as the wagons appeared and Fargo climbed onto the Ovaro.

"This gulley ought to keep you off the open plains till night," he told the general as the man rode to a halt. "Get the horses some water, too." He turned and started on and Alanna hurried after him, riding in silence till he halted at a small stream that crossed the dry gulley. He waited there, let the Ovaro drink until the others came up, and then he rode on again. This time Alanna stayed behind with the general, and Fargo rode to the end of the gulley, his eyes sweeping the ground as a matter of habit.

He emerged from the gulley and peered across the flatland in the lowering dusk. He saw nothing but plains and he rode on another mile and dismounted, unsaddled the Ovaro, and stretched out on the hard prairie grass. It was almost dark as the general arrived with the wagons, and Fargo got to his feet and watched Burt Roscoe place the wagons in a loose circle. Peering into the distance, he saw Sally halting at least a hundred and fifty yards back.

"Cold jerky tonight. We'll eat better when we get into the mountains and get some firewood," the general said.

The night came in fast and a three-quarter moon rose to bathe the plain in a pale white light. The very tall hand with the hostile eyes collected the tin plates the general had handed out, and Fargo saw the hostility was deep in the man's face. Skye took his bedroll and walked away from the camp to where he could see Sally's wagons in the distance; he started to undress and was down to just his trousers when he saw the slender figure come toward him.

Alanna halted and her eyes roved over the powerful beauty of his torso. "There's something I want to say and I don't know if there will be another chance."

"I'm listening," Fargo said.

"I've some money of my own back home, a fair amount. It's yours if you can find a way to turn my father back before this goes on too far," she said.

"You don't give up, do you?" Fargo said. "I suppose you figure this is a step up, bribes without the bullets."

Her mouth tightened. "We all make mistakes. Can't you forget that? I'm sorry."

"I take time to forget things," Fargo said. "Especially bullets."

"What about my offer just now?"

"Go to bed, honey," he said. "Unless you want to stay here."

"No, thank you," she snapped, spun on her heel, and stalked away.

Fargo shed his trousers and crawled into the bedroll as the night brought a sharp wind. He cast another glance at the two black shapes in the distance before he closed his eyes and let sleep blot out the world.

When the new day's sun slid over the plains, he woke, dressed quickly, and carried his bedroll back to where he'd left the Ovaro.

Alanna used her horse as a shield and finally emerged in a white shirt and black britches and she combed her raven locks with one hand. The general was the last up and took the longest to get himself together, Fargo noted.

"I'll ride on," Fargo said, and he put the Ovaro into a nice, easy trot across the flatland. He turned in the saddle to look back and saw the big Conestoga start to slowly roll forward, the other wagon and team following behind.

The land stayed flat, but he found a shallow dip, waited for the wagons to come into sight, and waved them forward. It was past noon when the dip of land came to an end and the wagons rolled back onto the prairie flatness. Sally continued to follow but stayed plenty far back. But the general stayed unhappy, Fargo saw by the glares the man shot behind his wagons. They'd reach the foothills of the mountains by sundown, Fargo estimated, and his eyes covered the ground as he rode. He'd seen only a few signs of Indian ponies, all old and dried prints, and it was midafternoon when the land began to lift in shallow rises. Alanna had spent the day riding with the wagons.

The Trailsman, perhaps a half-mile on ahead, felt a frown touch his brow as he caught the spiral of dust rising over a distant low hill. He spurred the Ovaro on as the column of dust grew higher and thicker.

More than one rider, he grunted silently. A lot more. He rode forward at an angle along the low hillside so he'd reach the crest without standing out like a crow on a fence, and he reined up as he saw the column of blue-clad cavalry troopers, some twenty of them, with an officer and a sergeant in the lead. He turned away and went back down the slope and saw the general and Alanna riding hard toward him.

"Just a cavalry platoon," he said.

"Damn," the general cursed. "They heading this way?"

"Yes," Fargo said with some surprise at the man's reaction.

"Find someplace. Get us out of sight," the general ordered.

"No real hiding place around here," Fargo said.

"There's got to be something, dammit," the man snapped, and started back to the wagons.

Fargo caught the faint smile on Alanna's lips as she turned and rode after her father, and he pushed his thoughts aside as he scanned the land. Another low rise a few hundred yards offered the only break in the flatland, and he put the Ovaro into a gallop, swept past the wagons, gestured with a wave, and saw the four heavy drays begin to turn and follow him. He saw the drivers go to their whips and the horses respond. Fargo slowed as he neared the top of the rise and let the others catch up. In the distance, Sally was following, still hanging back but hurrying to stay with them.

"What've you got against the cavalry, General?" Fargo asked.

"Nothing, but I don't want any news going back anywhere as to where I am. I told you, there are people in high places who want to stop me." The general frowned and Fargo watched the four wagons roll down the slope to the bottom of the dip of land.

"They're bound to see the wagon tracks," Fargo commented.

"Lots of wagon tracks out here. They might go right on by," the general answered.

"Then we'd best stop right here and be quiet," Fargo said, and saw the general frown as Sally drove her two wagons into the hollow.

''That goddamn girl brings them in here I'll have her hide,'' the general growled.

''She's stopping,'' Fargo said. ''Everybody stays here while I have a look.'' He sent the Ovaro up the slope at a walk. As he neared the top, he slid to the ground and continued the rest of the way on foot. Flattening himself on the ground when he reached the top of the slope, he saw the cavalry troop passing a few hundred yards away. He watched them ride across the wagon tracks, waited as they continued on, and finally slid backward until he was far enough from the top to get to his feet. He led the Ovaro back to where the general waited beside the four big drays, and he saw the nervousness in the man's wide face.

''Well?'' Taylor questioned.

''They're riding on,'' Fargo said, and saw relief flood the general's face. ''But you'd best give them time to put some distance on. I'd say wait right here another fifteen minutes.''

''Yes, whatever you think best,'' the general said, and turned away.

Fargo's glance went to Alanna and saw her face was a coolly impassive mask. He peered beyond to where Sally sat quietly atop the driver's seat of the Conestoga. He let the time go by and finally nodded to Burt Roscoe, who sat his horse nearby.

''Roll,'' he murmured, sending the Ovaro forward at a walk. Alanna rode beside her father only a few yards behind him and the wagons followed closely. He saw Sally start to roll forward, carefully keeping her distance. At the far end of the shallow dip of land the slope rose in a slow incline and he took the Ovaro upward and had just reached the top when he reined in abruptly.

''Shit,'' he spat out as his eyes moved along the line of blue-clad horsemen that stretched across the ground. They had plainly been waiting, he saw, and his glance fastened on the captain in the center of the line. He took in a young face, not enough years on it to put any harsh lines on yet, but the captain had more astuteness than his age showed. He had seen the wagon tracks and decided not to follow them into the hollow and perhaps find himself in a chase. Instead, he'd gone on and doubled back in a wide circle to wait for the wagons to emerge from the hollow of land.

The general rode over the top of the slope, Alanna beside him and the wagons close behind.

"Surprise," Fargo said blandly, and watched ths shock flood the man's face.

"Dammit, you said they went on," the general hissed.

"Seems I was wrong," Fargo said, and watched the captain motion his troop forward as Sally's wagons came in sight and halted at once. The captain reined up in front of the general.

"Captain Jonathan Oster, Platoon B, U.S. Fifth Cavalry," he said. "Are those your wagons?"

"The four drays are mine," the general said.

"What are you carrying?" Captain Oster asked.

"Shale," the general answered.

"We'll have to examine them," the captain said.

"What in hell for?" General Taylor roared.

"You could be smuggling contraband, whiskey, rifles, stolen army supplies, anything. There's been a lot of smuggling through here."

"That's ridiculous. They're carrying shale. You can see it, for God's sake," General Taylor barked.

"We'll find out, sir," Captain Oster said with polite firmness. He snapped commands to his men and Fargo moved back as ten troopers dismounted and began to take the tarpaulins from the four wagons. Four more troopers came with short-handled shovels and began to dig into the shale and toss it on the ground.

"Goddammit, that's my property," the general roared.

"We'll reload whatever we take off, sir," said Captain Oster with cool authority, and he dismounted to walk around the four big drays as his men continued to shovel the shale out of the first wagon. They had emptied the wagon of three-quarters of its contents when the captain called a halt. He leaned into the wagon, his eyes probing into the shale still remaining in place. He took out his heavy, army-issue Smith & Wesson revolver and, holding it by the barrel, began to tap the floorboards of the wagon with the butt. He moved carefully from one side of the wagon to the other, and when he finished, he had one of the troopers crawl under the wagon with him as he plainly continued to look for a false floor. Finally, Captain Oster pushed himself out from under the wagon and ordered his men to begin unloading the second wagon.

"You're wasting your time and mine, too, goddammit," Taylor boomed out.

"Sorry," the young captain said, and continued to keep his men unloading the second wagon.

Fargo dismounted and stretched his long frame out on the ground, and he saw Alanna do the same. He met her glance for an instant and her eyes held something close to mocking triumph before she looked away. Fargo relaxed on his elbows as Captain Oster gave the second wagon the same searching examination he had the first and then turned to the remaining two drays. When he finally finished, the captain stood back for a moment, took another searching walk around each of the wagons, and finally ordered the rest of his troopers to help reload the wagons bare-handed.

The day was well into afternoon when the task was finished and the general's face resembled the color of the sun that moved across the sky.

"This is inexcusable," General Taylor snapped. "I'm going to have you brought up on charges for this, Captain."

"You do that, sir," Captain Oster said, and swung onto his brown gelding. "Column forward," he sang out, and the platoon swung smartly in behind him as he rode away.

Fargo stood up and watched the platoon recede into the distance and a furrow pressed itself deep into his brow.

"Put those tarpaulins back on," General Taylor ordered his crew, and Fargo moved the Ovaro closer to him.

"Something strange about this, I'd say," Fargo murmured.

"Such as?" the general snapped.

"The captain rode away without so much as a look at Sally Jamison's wagons," Fargo commented.

"Shows he's not very thorough," the general growled.

"He was damn thorough when he went over your wagons," Fargo returned blandly.

"I certainly can't explain the actions of some apple-cheeked boy captain," the man tossed back, and it was plain he wasn't about to say anything more.

Fargo waited to one side, and when the tarpaulins were back in place, he waved the wagons forward. He let thoughts tumble through his mind as he rode. The entire incident with the army platoon hadn't set right. The captain had been waiting to halt the general's wagons. The search had been selective and deliberate. But why? he pondered. What did they expect to find? Somebody believed the general was carrying more than oil shale to New Mexico. Unless—and he couldn't rule out the possibility—the captain had found the wrong wagons. He could have been out to intercept four other wagons. Fargo grimaced at the thought. It would have been a hell of a coincidence, he grunted. He pushed aside further speculation and brought his concentration back to the land.

The foothills of the Sangre de Cristo range appeared directly ahead and the Trailsman saw the trails of unshod Indian ponies that began to crisscross the ground, most of them fairly recent. His eyes followed the broad swath of a slain deer that had been dragged behind one of the ponies, and he lifted his gaze to sweep the land that lay before him. But he saw no bronzed horsemen and nothing else to cause alarm and he kept the wagons moving forward until the fading dusk brought them just within range of the foothills.

Fargo decided to camp out on the flatland and waved the wagons to a halt. As Burt Roscoe brought the big drays into a loose circle Fargo's gaze went to where Sally brought her wagons to a stop. The general had dismounted and one of Roscoe's men had begun to open cans of beans.

Fargo wandered over to where the general was unsaddling his horse. "More than enough Indian pony tracks," Fargo remarked. "I think it'd be a nice gesture if you asked the Jamison girl to camp closer for the night."

"I'm not interested in nice gestures. She stays the hell away from my wagons, you hear me?" the general shot back, and Fargo nodded and turned away, his lips pursed. He didn't expect any real trouble yet, not out here in the flatland. Apache didn't like attacks across flat ground. But the general's vehemence had taken him by surprise. The man seemed to have some kind of obsession about his wagons and their cargo. Or he was the kind who felt that everyone was out to do him in. He'd have to change his attitude before the trip was over, Fargo reflected, taking the tin plate of beans and cold beef one of the men handed him.

He ate quickly, brought his plate back to the cook, and returned to the Ovaro in the dim moonlight to find Alanna waiting there. Her lovely features held a coolly smug smile. "You believe me now, Fargo?" she asked.

"I'm beginning to wonder more."

"Is that all?" the young woman flared. "Good God, wasn't it obvious enough that they knew?"

"Knew what?" Fargo questioned.

"What I told you. The real reason he's going to New Mexico. That cavalry troop was under orders. They were looking for him," Alanna said.

"It seemed so," Fargo agreed.

"They knew the damn shale was just a cover."

"Cover for what?" Fargo asked.

"Whatever." Alanna shrugged. "They probably expected he was bringing money in the wagons to help finance his takeover."

Fargo let his lips purse. Her suppositions made sense, but once again, they didn't fit right. "But they didn't find anything," he reminded her. "Why not?"

"I don't know why not, dammit," Alanna said, her voice tight with frustration and anger.

"Maybe that means they were wrong and so are you," Fargo said. "Maybe Washington got hold of nothing more than rumors. Hell, that's sure happened before. Maybe the oil-shale venture is the real reason he's going."

"No, no, no, dammit," Alanna said, shaking her raven locks vigorously. "It's a cover, somehow, someway. He's going down to start the Republic of New Mexico."

"You've no proof, honey," Fargo said, not ungently.

"I know. I heard enough, listening to him planning with his friends," she said. "Only you won't believe me, damn you. You don't care if he rots in prison or is killed."

"I believe what I see," Fargo said. "They searched and didn't find anything. You've got nothing to support your words. You could be plain wrong, as I said, or playing your own game."

"Go to hell," Alanna flung at him, spun on her heel, and strode away to be quickly swallowed up in the darkness.

Fargo pulled himself onto the Ovaro and his lips were drawn back in distaste. He'd told it to her as he saw it and he'd not take anything back, but he wasn't satisfied with his own words. Taking the four wagons through the mountain range still didn't make sense. It just wasn't reason enough for the risk involved, and Fargo heard his own whispered oath. Dammit, the man was hiding something. He was playing some kind of game and the stakes had to be damn high. Alanna's explanation would fit, Fargo realized. But no doubt a lot of other things might also, he grunted. Only one thing was certain so far: The United States cavalry had been waiting and they'd made their search and found nothing. He'd stay with that until something more appeared.

He slowly rode the Ovaro the hundred yards to where Sally Jamison's wagons were still and dark. He halted and lifted his voice in a soft call. "You still up?" he asked. His eyes were on the Conestoga but it was the canvas of the Owensboro Texas wagon that lifted and a round-cheeked face with short, blond hair peered out at him with a bright smile.

"I am," the face said.

"Me too," a second voice added, and another face popped out from beneath the flap of canvas.

Fargo stared at the two girls. They weren't twins, he found himself thinking, but they might almost have been except that the second one's cheeks weren't as round and her blond hair was a fraction longer.

"Who the hell are you?" Fargo heard himself ask in astonishment.

"I'm Elsa," the first one said.

"I'm Eva," the second chimed in.

"I'm shit-assed surprised," Fargo muttered.

5

Fargo stared at the two girls—each about twenty, he guessed—and they looked back at him from the wagon with cheerful smiles. Astonishment continued to be a small cyclone inside him and it took him a moment to find his voice again. "Where's Sally Jamison?" he asked.

"She'll be right back. She went to throw the dinner scraps away so's they won't attract animals to the wagons," the one called Elsa answered.

"I'll try again," Fargo rasped. "Who the hell are you two?"

"We're Sally's cousins," Eva answered, and she stood up inside the wagon. She had round, apple-shaped busts that matched her cheeks, Fargo saw, and they jiggled as she climbed out of the wagon. The other one followed and Fargo saw that she, too, had round busts that jiggled in unison. He took both girls in as they faced him side by side. They fairly burst with a very definite physical vitality and their bright smiles were as much invitation as innocence, he decided. They appraised him with an open appreciation that bordered on flirtation.

"This explains all the laundry," Fargo said through gritted teeth.

"What?" Elsa frowned.

"Never mind," Fargo muttered, and heard the footsteps coming around the Conestoga. He glared at the small, tight figure with the light-brown hair and saw

Sally stop in surprise, her glance going to the two girls at once.

"Dammit, what are you two doing out here?" she yelled.

"We told you we were tired of being cooped up," Eva said, pouting. "Besides, you know we had to come out sooner or later."

"When I said so," Sally snapped, and brought her eyes back to Fargo's face.

"You're even crazier than I thought," Fargo told her.

"It had to be," Sally said. "I figured there'd be no chance of your helping me if you knew about Eva and Elsa."

"You're sure as hell right about that," Fargo barked. "Why? What in hell are they doing out here with you?"

"Eva and Elsa were raised by my folks. They want to find out what happened to them as much as I do. Besides, I couldn't leave them alone."

"So you brought them out to get killed along with yourself. That makes a lot of sense," Fargo said, and shook his head as the astonishment still clung to him.

"What brought you visiting?" Sally questioned.

"Came to tell you I saw plenty of Indian pony prints. You have trouble, fire a shot and I'll come running," Fargo said.

"That's real sweet of you, Fargo," Elsa said.

"Real sweet," Eva agreed, and both looked across at Sally.

"His conscience is bothering him," Sally returned. "He could've had us up there with the other wagons."

"Damn, you're a stubborn package," Fargo cut in.

"Well, it's true," she flared.

"I've said my piece and I'll be going now," Fargo told her. "But I'd not go wandering away to throw out garbage." He started to turn the Ovaro away when Elsa called out.

"You come visit again, Fargo," she said, and there was more than politeness in her voice.

"You do that," Eva agreed, and he saw their almost identical blue eyes glistening with the invitation.

"I just might," Fargo said, and hurried away. He returned to where the four big drays were silent, dark bulks, found a spot a half-dozen yards from them, and bedded down. He went to sleep with astonishment still wrapped around him like an invisible blanket. But the night stayed still and he woke to the morning sun, used his canteen to wash, and saw some of Burt Roscoe's men staring across the land to where Elsa and Eva were now plainly visible beside Sally's wagons. Fargo walked the Ovaro to where a mug of coffee waited, and the general, Alanna following, hurried over to him.

"Where'd those other two come from?" Taylor barked.

"Seems they were there all along," Fargo said. "They're cousins, all out to find out what happened to their folks."

"I don't like it, not one damn bit. They'll only cause trouble," the general said. "You tell that Jamison girl I don't want her following me any longer."

"She won't listen to that. As she said, it's a free country. She can go wherever she likes," Fargo reminded him.

"We'll see about that," the general muttered, and stalked away and Fargo's eyes went to Alanna. She looked uncomfortable and allowed a small shrug.

"Daddy's always been a stubborn, hot-tempered man," she said.

"I hope he reins in. I'd hate to see him do anything stupid," Fargo said. He turned away and saw Burt Roscoe and the other men watching. "Let's roll," he told them, and climbed onto the Ovaro.

He rode to the front and waited for the wagons to come into line and the general, Alanna beside him, to

71

fall in beside the first dray. Fargo saw Sally driving the Conestoga, but the Owensboro had been detached and Elsa held the reins. He turned the pinto and set off in a trot, the mountain range rising before him. He found a wide pathway that led up into the foothills and waved the wagons forward before riding on. The terrain turned quickly to mountain brush, good red cedar and spruce, with plenty of serviceberry and some Rocky Mountain maple. But the unshod Indian pony prints became more frequent. Different hunting parties, he decided. Probably different tribes.

The wide passage began to narrow and grow steeper and he pushed through a growth of red cedar to find a long, clear slope. He returned to the passage until the wagons rolled up. "Hack your way through here, about a quarter of a mile," he told the general.

The men took axes from one of the packhorses. They began to chop a passage through the cedar, hacking off low, thin branches mostly until they had enough room for the wagons to go through single-file. But it had taken time and the sun was in the noon sky when the wagons rolled onto the clear slope where only a few tall spruce dotted the land.

Fargo glance back to see Sally emerging from the passageway with the Conestoga.

"Goddamn her. She's got no right to take advantage of our sweat," the general spit out.

"You make a path, anybody can use it," Fargo remarked.

"Goddamm it, you taking her side, Fargo?" General Taylor questioned angrily.

"No, just pointing out facts," Fargo said, and sent the pinto forward. He stayed at a trot up the slope and heard Alanna hurrying to catch up to him.

"Daddy's very tense," she said as she came alongside. "He's not always this inhospitable."

"That's nice," Fargo said blandly.

"That Jamison girl really thinks she can find out what happened to her folks up here?" Alanna asked.

"She must, for all the effort and danger she's taking," Fargo said.

"You think she can?" Alanna asked.

He shrugged. "Not likely, but it's possible. There are plenty of prospectors in these mountains. One might know something. Then she could find some signs that'd tell her more than she wants to know."

"Signs? You mean remains," Alanna said.

"Whatever." He shrugged and crested the top of the slope. The land leveled out and became wooded at once, with small hills and dips all heavily covered by trees. He moved forward slowly and halted to bend low from the saddle. He scooped up a piece of anklet, hide-backed, decorated with designs etched into the leather. "Apache," he grunted. "Mescalero." He tossed the torn anklet aside and moved forward, searched the terrain, and found a curving trail the wagons would be able to negotiate.

"You think the Apache know we're here?" Alanna asked.

"The ones up on that hill to the right do," Fargo said, and her eyes widened in alarm as she peered up the hillside.

"I don't see anything," Alanna said.

"I don't see them, either, but they're there. You don't see Apache until you don't want to see them."

"Then how do you know they're there?" Alanna frowned.

"Leaves, brush, grouse taking off suddenly," Fargo said. "A small party, not more than five or six, I'd guess."

"How in heavens do you know that?" she asked.

"Watched a line of brush move and counted how long it took them to pass by," Fargo said. "Let's go back and get the others." He turned the Ovaro and rode off, Alanna close at his heels, and when he led the wagons forward again, the day had begun to wane. He found a clearing large enough to hold all four drays and brought them in for the night.

"Alanna tells me you saw signs of Mescalero," the general said as he dismounted, and Fargo nodded. "You don't figure they'll hit us soon, do you?"

"Not likely. They'll watch and see, first. They might make a raid but nothing full-scale yet," Fargo said.

The general moved away and Fargo watched Sally and the two other girls halt their wagons alongside the curving trails, still keeping at least a hundred yards away. He unsaddled the Ovaro as the dusk began to slide into dark, and he had walked toward the cook when he slid into the shadows and halted. Burt Roscoe and three of his men were talking, their eyes on the Conestoga, and as he watched, he saw the general pause beside the men. They spoke to him in quick, muttered tones and Fargo saw him turns his palms up.

"That's between you and the men, Burt," Fargo heard the general say. "I don't want to know anything." Morton Taylor walked quickly away and Fargo's smile was tight. The general was being clever. He wanted the benefits without the blame.

Fargo strolled forward, took a plate of food from the cook, and sat down to finish it as night descended. When he handed the plate back, he made a wide circle around the wagons and, staying in the tree cover, silently moved to where Sally and her cousins had halted. He slid to the ground when he was close and saw Elsa vigorously drying her hair. Or was it Eva? He frowned. She had taken her blouse off and a slip covered the very round breasts. They jiggled beautifully as she rubbed the towel over her hair, and when she finished, she disappeared into the Owensboro.

He stayed in place and Sally came from the Conestoga for a moment, peered into the distance toward the general's wagons, and then climbed back inside the wagon. He heard her undressing and he stayed in place and let his powerful frame relax against the stringy bark of a red cedar. He sat silent and still as a stone.

The moon rose to slowly slide its way across the sky and still he waited. The hour was nearing midnight when he first heard, then saw the four figures approaching the wagons. He picked out the very tall one first, the other three only passing faces to him. As he watched, the very tall one began to climb into the Conestoga, a second man following, while the other two made their way into the Owensboro. In seconds, Fargo heard muffled cries and the sounds of struggle, and he rose to his feet, unholstered the big Colt, and crept forward.

The tall one with the hostile eyes emerged from the Conestoga first, dragging Sally with him, while the second man held her by the arms. The other two came from the second wagon, each holding his prize around the waist. Sally wore a flannel nightgown that revealed a long, lovely curve of leg as she tried a backward kick at the tall figure holding her.

"That's enough," the man said, and slapped her across the side of the face and she yelped in pain. He gazed down at her and a wolfish grin split his long, severe face. "You keep following us. That means you must be looking for company," he said.

"And that's what you're going to get," the man holding Eva chimed in. "Tonight and every night you follow us around. All the boys would like a piece of ass."

"Bastard," Eva shot back, trying to twist away, but he yanked her back by her short blond hair and she cried out in pain.

"Damn you," Fargo heard Sally swear, and he saw her spit in the thin, severe face.

"Bitch," the man snarled, but the act failed to make him let go. Instead, he flung her to the ground and pressed his heel against the back of her neck. "You're gonna be first, girlie," he threatened, and Fargo halted at the edge of the trees, the Colt raised in his hand. Maybe they'd back off if they were challenged. Then maybe they wouldn't. It was a chance he'd have to take.

"Let them go," he said loudly and firmly and he saw the four men spin their glances in the direction of his voice. He stepped forward far enough so they could at least see the dark outline of his body. "It's me, Fargo," he said. "Let them go."

"Get your ass out of here, Fargo," the tall one said tersely. "Mind your own damn business. You break trail. We'll break tail," he added, and his laugh was a harsh, mirthless sound.

"Let go and get back to camp," Fargo said. "Don't lose your job the hard way."

He saw the tall one's hostile face turn even colder. "The general thinks he needs you," the man said. "I'm gonna show him he's wrong." Fargo saw the man's long, bony arm flash downward to his holster. His shot was instant and the tall, thin figure suddenly seemed to be a long-legged puppet jiggling on an invisible wire. With a motion awkward even in death, the man collapsed, but Fargo's second shot rang out before the figure hit the ground. The second man had cleared his holster with his six-gun when he took the force of the big Colt's bullet full in the chest. He flew backward to land in a heap on the ground with a final twitching gasp.

Fargo saw Elsa tear out of the grip of the man holding her and fling herself face forward on the ground, but Fargo held his fire for a moment. The man dropped his hands to his sides, his face ashen as he knew death stared at him through the barrel of the big Colt.

"No, don't shoot . . ." he muttered, backing away.

Fargo's glance flicked to the last man, who still held Eva in front of him. The man tried to bargain, his voice tight with fear.

"You'll hit her," he said.

"And you," Fargo said flatly, and saw the man swallow hard, take his arm from around Eva, and stand very still. "That was the only smart thing you did tonight. Start walking," he ordered, gesturing to the other man with his Colt. Both had their backs to him and were walking away from the wagons when he swung onto the Ovaro and fell in behind them. The others were up and awake when he herded the two men to the wagons, Alanna in a light robe standing near her father, Burt Roscoe to one side.

"What's all this?" the general asked.

"Little change in your plans," Fargo said.

"I didn't have any plans," General Taylor protested.

"But you were happy to look the other way," Fargo said. His eyes went to Burt Roscoe and they were cold as an ice floe in January. "There are two waiting to be buried. You can go get them," Fargo said. The man turned away and muttered orders to three of his hands.

"You saying you killed two of my men, Fargo?" the general barked.

"No, they got themselves killed," Fargo answered.

"Dammit, I can't afford to lose even one man, much less two." The general frowned.

"The price of looking the other way," Fargo said, and moved the Ovaro on, slowing as he passed Alanna and met her eyes. She held his glance for a moment before looking away with discomfort in the black orbs. He rode on and knew she'd not make excuses for the general this time, and he gave her credit for that. He moved a distance upland, found a patch of spruce, and bedded down for what was left of the night.

The morning came on a bright sun. Everyone was awake and ready to move when he came down to the wagons. Alanna's black hair glistened in the new sun, but she was plainly more subdued than he'd ever seen her and she fell in beside the general in silence as he moved the drays forward.

Fargo threw a glance back and saw Sally starting to move the Conestoga forward, Eva and Elsa on the Owensboro. He rode ahead and crisscrossed east and west twice before finding a circuitous passage south that had once been a moose trail, he imagined. It was single-file for the big drays and slow traveling, and he went on, his eyes sweeping the terrain. He spotted Indian pony tracks, none very old, and caught a glimpse of two near-naked horsemen, each wearing brow bands that held back stringy black hair. "Mescalero," Fargo muttered, and watched the two Apache vanish into the high trees.

He rode on, held a steady pace, and called a halt twice to let the horses drink at mountain streams. Alanna continued to stay back with her father when Fargo rode on, and the day began to wind itself down. Fargo found a hollow and reined to a halt, waited until the drays rolled up, and waved them to a halt.

One of the men had shot a pair of fat grouse and the others began to make a fire at once. The two that had visited Sally kept their distance from him, Fargo saw, quickly looking away when they saw his eyes on them. They'd learned a lesson, he was certain, and he took the Ovaro to one side, unsaddled the horse, and folded himself on the ground to wait for the birds to finish roasting.

Sally had pulled up a good hundred yards back, he noted before the night descended to cloak the land. The light from the small fire cast a flickering orange-yellow glow and he watched a slender figure walk toward him.

Alanna halted, the firelight behind her, the long line of her breasts silhouetted in a lovely curve. "I tried to convince father to let the Jamison girls camp with us tonight," she said. "He wouldn't hear of it."

"Trying to make amends for him for last night?" Fargo asked, and her features tightened at once.

"Trying to do the right thing," she said, the answer oblique.

"It doesn't work," Fargo said, and she frowned back. "People have to make their own amends. Nobody can do it for them."

She shrugged and a moment of pain touched the black eyes. "I'm still right about everything else," she said. "You'll see." She turned and strode away.

Fargo watched her hips move under her riding britches, narrow and tight and somehow combining provocativeness and propriety. He sat back, rose to get some of the grouse when the birds were finally roasted, and as the moon rose higher, he took his bedroll and walked to a dark place halfway between the camp and Sally's wagons.

He had just undressed to his drawers and lay down on the bedroll when he heard the whispered call. "Fargo," the voice said, and he sat up, his hand around the Colt at once as he frowned into the brush. A bush moved and Elsa pushed her way into view. Just behind her, almost as if she were a shadow, was Eva.

They came forward to halt side by side in front of him. "We were on our way toward the general's camp when we saw you leave. We dropped into the brush and watched where you went," Elsa said.

Fargo's eyes moved over the two girls. Both wore loose housedresses and slippers. "Why were you going to the camp?" he asked.

"To find you. We want to thank you properly for last night," Eva said. She raised both arms and with a quick motion flung the dress over her head to stand naked in front of him, round apple-shaped breasts not large but very high and firm with surprisingly large pink nipples. Her body, slightly chunky, fairly throbbed with youthful vitality. She had a convex little belly, wide, rounded hips, and a densely curly bush at the triangle of her legs. The motion beside her took his eyes away and he watched Elsa fling her dress over

79

her head to stand equally naked, virtually a physical carbon copy of Eva, including the youthful vitality. They stepped forward together and Eva sank to her knees on one side of him, Elsa on the other.

"Sally know you're doing this?" Fargo asked.

"Good God, no!" Elsa giggled.

"She's against us giving anything away," Eva said.

"Meaning what exactly?" Fargo asked.

"She still hopes you'll get us to join in with the general's wagons. She's not about to put out until you do," Elsa said.

"What makes you think she'll put out then?" Fargo asked, his brows lifting.

"Maybe she won't. Sally's funny that way," Elsa said.

"Stuffy." Eva giggled and Elsa joined in, and Fargo watched their breasts jiggle tantalizingly and felt himself responding to the sight of their throbbing, exciting nakedness. Elsa's hands came forward, took his drawers, and pulled them from him and he knew his organ had popped upright with pulsating strength. "Oh, my," he heard Elsa breathe. "Yes, oh, yes," she said, and he felt her hand close around him as Eva came forward to push her lips over his mouth. Her tongue was an instant seeker, darting against his and he reached up and grasped hold of her very round breasts.

"Yes, yes," Eva said, and she lifted herself to push the smooth mounds into his face, found his mouth, and pressed each down as she gasped in pleasure. As he caressed and sucked the round breasts, he felt warm wonderful wetness engulf him as Elsa's lips found his shaft, a sweet, surging sensation that flooded over him.

Eva lifted her firm body higher, brought her round belly down over his face, rubbed it back and forth, and did the same with the densely curly triangle until she leaned back and brought the liquescent, soft lips to him, and he took of her as she screamed in pleasure. But even as he caressed and kissed, he felt Elsa straddle his hips and sink her dark, wet warmth over him, lifting and drawing down, slowly pumping, quickening at her own pace, and his maleness throbbed, soared, surged, and Elsa's cries joined Eva's in a sensuous symphony, each an echo of the other. They made robust, eager love to him with a rhythm that matched each other's, and when he felt his own ecstasy bursting forth, Elsa screamed and Eva joined the paean of rapture as they climaxed together.

Eva fell away from him, drawing her firm young legs up across his chest, while Elsa lay across his groin, gasping for breath, her face pressed against his still-tumescent maleness. They stirred, finally, Eva moving to lay against his right side and Elsa pulling herself up on his left.

"You two say thanks this way often?" Fargo inquired.

"Not often," Elsa said, giggling, and Eva echoed the little laugh.

Fargo felt both pairs of breasts move against his sides. They both smiled up at him with a wide-eyed, happy contentment that made them look like little girls that had found a new doll. They snuggled hard against him, arms crisscrossing his chest.

Finally Eva sat up. "We'd best get back," she said. "Sally's asleep by now." Elsa sat up and both found their housedresses and tossed them over their heads. They stood up and looked down at him with bright smiles. "Tomorrow night, maybe," Eva said.

"Maybe," Fargo agreed, and their smiles widened.

"The same but different," Elsa said. It was a promise sure to tease, they both knew, and they said as much with a flash of smugness. "Good night, Fargo," Elsa said.

"Good night," Eva added, and they both hurried away into the darkness.

Fargo lay back. This entire job was made of surprises, he murmured silently. But the surprises were improving and he was happy for that, he grunted, turned on his side, and went to sleep, satisfied and weary.

He woke with the morning sun, stretched, and found the events of the night were still clinging pleasantly. He rose and his eyes went to where the Conestoga and the Owensboro were lined up, one behind the other. He glimpsed Elsa and Eva, blond hair shining, as they hurried between wagons, and he saw Sally emerge in a green shirt and dark-green skirt. She busied herself hitching the horses to the Conestoga and he turned and strolled back to the general's camp. He accepted a cup of coffee and saw Taylor talking to Burt Roscoe.

Alanna came toward him from the other side, her lovely lips holding a cool smile. "Changed camps, have you, Fargo?" she asked, and he caught the edge of waspishness in her voice.

"Been sleepwalking, have you, Alanna?" he returned.

"I was restless and got up. I thought I might talk with you but you weren't around," she said almost crossly.

"I wasn't where you think," Fargo said. "You still want to talk, you can ride with me."

"No, the moment's passed. Maybe it was the restlessness and the night," she said, and swept passed him.

She hadn't been the only one restless, he reminded himself as he went on to saddle the Ovaro. He moved the wagons out and rode ahead, grimacing as he watched the terrain grow steeper, the ground growing into little more than a covering of uneven rock. Spurring the Ovaro forward, he took the horse still higher along the rocky footing and felt the pinto struggle to keep from slipping. He slowed, let the horse set its own pace, and finally reached the top of the steep rock climb. The land leveled off, hills reaching up on both sides of a high plateau that would make for good traveling despite the heavy tree cover. But the heavily loaded drays would never make the climb as they were, he realized, and he carefully took the Ovaro back down the steep and rock-covered passage.

The wagons had reached the start of the climb when he returned, and he reined up and watched the first dray move forward. The horses went perhaps a dozen yards before they began to slip on the rocks as they strained to pull their heavy loads. The driver went to the whip but the horses only slipped more as they tried to move without getting their feet firmly planted.

"Hell, we can't make this. You'll have to find another way, Fargo," General Taylor said.

"There is no other way," Fargo answered. " 'Less you want to take a month and cut down a spruce forest or try rolling your wagons along the side of a mountain."

"Goddamn, this is impossible," the man swore, staring at the heavy-breathing team of horses.

"It was your idea to take four heavily loaded drays through the mountains," Fargo said. He dismounted and walked to where Burt Roscoe sat his horse behind the first wagon. "Unhitch two of the other teams," Fargo said. "Bring them forward and harness them in front of this team."

"Three teams per wagon," Roscoe said.

"That's right. We bring the wagons up one at a time. That's the only way they'll make it," Fargo said, and Roscoe quickly moved to carry out his orders. When the three teams were harnessed together, Fargo stepped to one side and watched as they began to pull the big dray upward. The six horses still had to strain, but they could pull the load without slipping or bursting the veins in their legs. It was slow and hard forward motion, but the first dray finally reached the top, where it was pulled to one side and the three teams unharnessed and brought down to the second wagon. Once again, the six horses strained, but they moved the second dray across the slippery rocks and pulled it to the top. This time Fargo insisted on a half-hour's rest for the horses, and as he leaned against a tree, Alanna appeared, the black eyes moving over him with appraising admiration.

"You are the very best," she said.

"So they say," he agreed.

"You ever hear of being modest?" she said with an edge.

"Modesty is for those who need it," Fargo grunted. He turned from her and waved the men with the three teams down the slope.

The sun was in the afternoon sky when the last of the big drays made it to the top of the rocky passage, and as the men began to rehitch the teams, Fargo saw Sally start the climb below. The Conestoga wasn't as heavily loaded as were the four drays, but it was a more unwieldy wagon, designed for prairie travel not high mountain terrain. The Owensboro wasn't much better, even though it had a slightly lower center of gravity. He watched her start and saw her horses begin to flounder.

"I'll take one of those teams before you hitch them up again," Fargo said.

"Like hell," he heard the general bark. "Maybe we can finally get rid of her."

"Not here," Fargo said. "The Apache will be on them like hawks on a chicken coop."

"Nobody told them to follow me," the general said. "It's their risk."

Fargo shot a glance at Alanna and saw her look away, her face tight with uncomfortableness. He whirled the Ovaro and took the reins of one team of horses.

"You're working for me, Fargo, not them," the general shouted.

"You're paying me to break trail. You don't own me," Fargo said.

"You haven't heard the last of this, Fargo," General Taylor threatened, but he turned away and Fargo rode down the rock passage pulling the team along. The general would have turned to Burt Roscoe and the others, but he knew he was already shorthanded. He didn't dare risk losing still more men, Fargo smiled grimly. But the threat hadn't been an idle one. The general was not a man to forget. Fargo grunted in derision. He was losing respect for the man with every passing day, and he pushed away further thoughts as he reached Sally and the Conestoga.

He hitched the team in front of hers and the two teams moved forward with the wagon while Sally held the reins. When they reached the top, he brought the horses down for the Owensboro and pulled the wagon up with unexpected ease. Burt Roscoe and two of his men rode up, unhitched their team, and brought it back to the last dray. The other three drays were rolling on in the distance, Fargo saw, a gesture of disdain the general had flung back.

"Thank you, Fargo," Sally said gravely. "I owe you."

"But you still think I should've done more for you," Fargo said.

"Yes." She nodded, her chin lifted firmly.

"Good," Fargo said blandly. "I wouldn't want to see you go soft on me." He passed over Elsa and Eva with a glance as he rode away and saw the laughter in their eyes. He caught up to the four drays and went by the wagons and on ahead.

The relatively flat plateau stretched out in front of them and Fargo sent the Ovaro up a steep passage to the left where he threaded his way through narrow crevices to the top of a craggy peak. He halted on a ledge and frowned as he immediately picked up a trail of dust that rose skyward. He watched the plume moving along the way the wagons had traveled, still far in the distance. Dusk had begun to settle when he made

85

his way back down through the creviced passages. He swung onto the bottom flatland as the four drays rolled up and he motioned to a steep side of brush-covered land that rose up to form a green wall. The wagons pulled in to line up against it and Fargo peered into the distance to see Sally swing in and halt. She still kept her hundred yards back, he noted.

"We'll have company by morning. Riders following the way we came," Fargo said as the general dismounted, and he saw alarm flood the man's face at once.

"Apache?" Alanna asked.

"Too much dust for Apache," Fargo grunted. "I'd guess ten to fifteen riders, maybe more, moving hard."

"The army again?" The general frowned.

Fargo turned the question in his mind. It was possible. The army could be persistent. But they'd had their crack at the general. It was unlikely they'd come chasing all this distance for another. "I'd guess not," he said.

"Maybe they're not following us. Maybe they're just going the same way," the general said.

"Maybe," Fargo said, and turned away.

Alanna came up to him as he unsaddled the Ovaro. "You don't believe that, do you?" she asked.

"Prospectors ride alone and quiet. Big parties of riders wouldn't be in these mountains unless they were looking for some thing or some body."

She took in the reply and her black eyes held on him. "That was a nice thing you did back there," she said. "Are you sure Sally Jamison's nothing special to you?"

"I answered that," Fargo growled.

"I feel sorry for them. Maybe that's disloyal, but then, I can't feel loyal about this trip. I just want it stopped before it's too late. You'll go against him for

86

Sally Jamison and her cousins but not for me," Alanna said accusingly.

"It's their necks not their words that pulled on me," Fargo said.

Alanna's lips tightened and she strode away as night fell.

Fargo took his sleeping bag and once again bedded down in a spot halfway to the Conestoga. He lay awake, waited, and when the moon passed the midnight sky, he turned on his side and realized he was disappointed. He pulled sleep around himself and slumbered soundly until he woke with the morning sun. He rose, washed, rolled up his things, and trudged back to where he'd left the Ovaro. He was annoyed at himself for still feeling disappointed, and as the general took the time to have coffee, Fargo walked the Ovaro back to the Conestoga.

Elsa and Eva greeted him in skirts and the top halves of their slips. "Sally's still dressing," Elsa said.

"What happened last night?" he asked softly.

The two girls looked at each other with frowns. "Sally stayed up late. We thought she was going to go and thank you herself, so we went to sleep," Eva said.

"You thought wrong," Fargo bit out.

They made almost identical faces. "She's a hard-nose," Elsa said.

"And stuffy," Eva chimed in, and they both shrugged apologetically.

Fargo felt the laugh work up from inside him. "Guess I just wanted seconds," he said, and sent the Ovaro galloping back to where the four drays waited to roll on.

Alanna tossed him a glance that still held accusation and hurt in it as he rode past.

He sent the wagons forward along the plateau while he swerved and climbed one of the steep and narrow passages to higher ground. When he halted, he let his gaze sweep the terrain and found the spiral of dust was coming up fast behind them. The riders would catch up to them in another hour, he estimated, and he sent the Ovaro hurrying down to where the wagons rolled placidly along. He rode on ahead and scanned the land and saw where the plateau came to an end in a series of sharp hills, heavy spruce and red cedar stands, and some rock formations covered with fringe moss and mountain shrub. He spied an opening between two slabs of rock large enough for the wagons and reined to a halt till they rolled up.

"Put the drays in there, two on one side and two on the other," Fargo said. "Company ought to be here any minute."

"Do it," the general barked, and Fargo watched Burt Roscoe direct the wagons into place and then put his men with rifles in hand behind and alongside the drays.

Fargo turned the Ovaro, spurred the horse up a steep crevice, and halted only a few yards up where a bower of trees let him look down at the scene below. His guess had been close enough as, within ten minutes, he saw the horsemen galloping along the plateau. He counted twelve riders led by a man wearing a stained yellow kerchief around his neck. Above the kerchief Fargo saw a hard face with a slash of a mouth and a twisted nose, and he watched as the man came to a halt in front of where the general waited, with Alanna alongside him.

"You must be Taylor," the man said.

"I am. And you?" the general answered.

"Name don't matter," the man said. "Call me Harry."

Fargo watched the man's eyes go to the four drays and a mirthless smile crossed his face. Sally had pulled her wagons to one side a hundred yards back and the man threw a glance at them before returning his eyes to the general.

"I'd like to do this the easy way," he said. "That way nobody gets hurt."

"Do what?" the general snapped.

"I want those wagons," Harry said.

Fargo heard the snort that fell from his lips. "This is where I came in," he muttered.

6

"There's nothing in those wagons you'd want. I'm carrying oil shale," the general said.

"I heard you're carrying a load piss-full of money," Harry said. "And we're taking it."

"You heard all wrong. There's no money in my wagons. A troop of U.S. cavalry searched them and all they found was my oil shale," Taylor said.

"We'll search better," Harry said. "What about that Conestoga and the Owensboro back there?"

"They're not with me," the general answered.

Harry allowed another icy smile. "Try again. They've been following right along with you," he said. His eyes flicked over the wagons again. "Tell your boys to step away from those wagons, now," he ordered.

"Or what?" the general blustered.

"There's going to be helluva gunfight and I'll still wind up with the wagons," Harry said. "I'll start by putting a bullet through the little lady next to you."

Fargo drew the big Sharps from its saddle holster, raised the rifle to his shoulder, and took aim. He pressed the trigger gently and Harry's hat blew from his head as the shot reverberated through the hills. The man ducked in automatic reaction as his hat skittered through the air.

"That wouldn't be nice, Harry," Fargo said, and the man straightened in the saddle and peered up into the trees, his face dark with surprise and anger. Fargo's eyes flew to the last rider in the group as he caught the flick of motion. He saw the man yank his six-gun out and Fargo fired the rifle again. The man buckled in two as he fell sideways from his horse. "That was real dumb of him, wasn't it, Harry?" Fargo called down.

Harry's eyes had become narrowed slits as he stared up at the bower of trees. "Who're you?" the man rasped.

"Names don't matter," Fargo said. "You still want to start that gunfight, Harry? There could be ten of us up here."

The man's face took on a sneer. "And maybe there's just you."

"But maybe I'm as good as ten men," Fargo replied, and Harry's eyes stayed slitted. "The general was telling the truth. There's no money in those wagons. You just go on back and forget you were here . . . before I make a mistake and put your head where your hat is."

Harry shot a glance at his hat lying a half-dozen feet away on the ground, and his mouth became even more of a thin slash. Slowly, the man turned his horse and moved toward his men. He leaned from the saddle to scoop up his hat and push it back on his head. He rode on, and his men followed in behind him and two paused to pick up the lifeless form on the ground.

Fargo watched them pass Sally's wagons and disappear down a dip in the plateau. He waited, made certain they were going on, and came down from the trees when the sound of their horses vanished from earshot.

"Think they've given up?" General Taylor asked.

Fargo's snort was a harsh and derisive sound. "They'll take some time to think, but that's all," he said. "Let's roll and find someplace better." He moved to one side as the men began to move the wagons forward, and he looked back to see Sally pulling the Conestoga out. He sent the pinto ahead through a curving trail so heavily covered with foliage he had to duck his head in places. But the wagons managed to clear the lowest of the branches and the mountain forest became cool and shaded.

Harry and his men would have no trouble picking up the wagon tracks, Fargo realized, and his eyes searched the terrain for a place to make a stand. The dense forest offered a kind of protection, but it also offered too much cover for anyone approaching and he was glad to see it suddenly end, the low-roofed trail opening onto an area of rock-bound ledges and spruce stands. His eyes scanned the land and spotted a place where rocks and trees came together to form a half-circle with a wall of stone at the back.

"Over there." He motioned to Burt Roscoe, and the man lined the four drays against the wall. The sun, no longer filtered through the thick forest foliage, burned down with midafternoon hotness, and Fargo waited for Sally to appear in the Conestoga. She finally came into sight and halted, keeping back, and he rode over to her and saw Elsa and Eva lean from the driver's seat of the Owensboro.

"Pull your wagons alongside those trees over there," Fargo said. "Then get out and take cover up in the brush. They may come in pouring lead into everything and everyone in sight, figuring they'll take out at least some of us."

Sally nodded and steered the Conestoga toward the line of trees. "Who are they?" she asked.

"Hijackers."

"What do they want?" she asked.

"They think the general's carrying money," Fargo told her. "They want the wagons." She nodded and brought the Conestoga to a halt, and Eva and Elsa pulled up close behind. "All of you stay under cover until it's over, you understand?" Elsa and Eva nodded in unison and Sally agreed with her silence. She swung her tight, neat figure to the ground and he rode back to the four drays.

The general was waiting impatiently. "You've some ideas to share with us?" he snapped sarcastically.

"A few," Fargo answered calmly. "Leave no more than three men with the wagons. We want them to see somebody. Everybody else get on those rocks in back. I expect they'll come shooting and charging, out to fill the wagons full of holes. You wait till I fire and then pour it down on them."

Burt Roscoe nodded and chose three men to stay with the wagons. They crouched behind the tarpaulin-covered sides while he went up into the spruce with everyone else. Fargo followed and swung from the Ovaro a dozen yards from the others, who had formed a loose line. He took the big Sharps and lowered himself to the ground where he could see the wagons below and the approach to them. Footsteps made him glance up and he saw Alanna carrying a .44-caliber Henry. She lowered herself to the ground beside him and tossed him a glance that carried grimness and triumph.

"You believe me now?" she asked.

"Nope," Fargo said, and drew a gasp of exasperation.

"Dammit, what more do you want?" Alanna said. "Even these cutthroats know the oil shale is just a cover."

"Because they're here for the wagons?" Fargo returned. "All that proves is that they heard the same rumor the army heard. Rumors travel hard and fast and they acted on it. I've seen rumors start gold rushes and panics."

"What's it take to get to you?" Alanna thrust angrily.

"Proof. Not rumors, not words. Proof. The army followed through and didn't find anything," he reminded her.

"I don't have an answer for that, dammit."

"Come see me when you do," Fargo said, dismissal in his tone as well as his words.

"You'll see," Alanna murmured and stretched out on her stomach, the rifle held to her shoulder.

Fargo glanced at the sky. The sun had begun to slip down toward the horizon line. They'd be coming soon, he was certain, and it was only a few minutes later when he heard the thunder of hoofbeats. He saw Alanna lift herself to her elbows, her finger on the trigger.

"Not till I fire," he reminded her, and she answered without looking up.

"I can remember," she muttered, and Fargo brought his gaze back to the ground below. Sally, Elsa, and Eva would stay hidden away, he was reasonably certain. The band of horsemen burst into view in moments, six-guns in hand, rifles at their shoulders. As he expected, they laid down a withering barrage of fire at the wagons, raking the Conestoga and Owensboro as they swept by and pouring lead over, into, and under the four drays.

Harry had wheeled around on the far side so Fargo picked a closer target and fired the rifle. The rider flew from his horse with a flapping of arms and legs. Alanna fired beside him and Fargo heard the others lay down a fusillade of shots. Roscoe's men were no sharpshooters and the riders below were fast-moving, racing targets, but Fargo saw three of the horsemen go down. As the rest scattered, he saw Harry in the distance, the stained yellow kerchief easy to see, and the man shouted as he waved frantically at his men. Harry had seen enough. He wasn't about to risk losing more of his men and he raced into the trees, the others following.

"That's it?" Alanna wondered, and sounded disappointed.

"For now," Fargo said. "Harry's already down by

94

four men. He doesn't want to lose any more and he knows he sure as hell would if he tried another charge here." Fargo rose to his feet and extended a hand to Alanna, but she pushed herself up and he smiled inwardly.

"But you think he'll try again," Alanna asked as she walked beside him down from the tree cover.

"Probably," Fargo said. "But he'll wait for someplace else, I'd guess." He reached the wagons as the others emerged from the trees, and the general tossed an apprehensive glance his way. "No more charges here," Fargo said. "This is as good a spot as any to stay the night. Bed down behind the wagons." He looked out across the distance to see Sally, Elsa, and Eva returning to their wagons.

As the cook warmed beans and johnnycakes and the dusk drifted down, Fargo's eyes scanned the surrounding land with its high crags and spruce that climbed the hillsides like so many silent soldiers. Harry could have crept back up on high and watched them make camp, Fargo knew, and he wasn't happy with the thought. But there was little he could do about it, and the darkness would shroud everything soon enough. He took a plate of food, ate slowly, and when he finished, he passed the general with his empty plate.

"How come everybody seems to think you're carrying money?" he asked. "First the army, now these jokers."

"How do I know?" Taylor answered, defensive at once. "I'm thinking maybe somebody deliberately started that rumor, figuring it'd put a stop to me one way or another."

Fargo turned the answer in his mind. It wasn't impossible, he concluded, and he turned his plate in as darkness descended to blanket the land with its blackness. It'd be a few hours before the moon rose high enough to slide around the high crags, he knew, and he took his bedroll and once again moved to a spot halfway to the Conestoga. He undressed to his drawers, lay down, and let the night wind cool his body. He stretched and knew there'd be a wait, but he felt certain he'd have a visit this night. Elsa and Eva? he pondered. Sally Jamison wasn't the visiting kind, it seemed, though her amber eyes could hold veiled promises.

He closed his eyes, let himself catnap, and listened to the night sounds, his senses never fully at rest. The moon had reached the top edge of a high peak when he heard the sound of brush moving below, unsure footsteps moving through the foliage.

He rose on one knee and peered down to see the two figures pushing through brush. "Up here," he called softly, and they halted, turned, and hurried up to him. Elsa and Eva were already wreathed in happy smiles that were full of anticipation when they reached him, their eyes moving across his muscled body. As one, they tossed aside their housedresses and almost rushed at him, pressed their firm nakedness against him. He fell back on the bedroll and they came with him, little giggly sounds from each, and this time it was Elsa who pressed her lips against him and quickly moved to offer one apple-round, firm breast. He felt Eva sliding herself over his groin, pushing her breasts against him, touching first one nipple and then the other to his quickly rigid shaft. The same but different, Elsa had said last time, and he reached down and cupped one hand around her concave belly, slid downward to press against the rounded pubic mound. Eva's tongue had just begun to trace a fiery path along his groin when the shot split the night and he heard the distant shouts.

"Damn," he said, and sat up, and Eva and Elsa went rolling to the sides. Another shot came from the campsite and Fargo yanked on jeans and gun belt and raced through the pale moonlight toward the drays. He saw the general first, then Burt Roscoe, and both men stared into the blackness.

"They took Alanna," the general said. "Goddammit, they took my daughter."

Fargo shot a hard glance at Burt Roscoe. "We bedded down back of the wagons the way you said," Roscoe told him. "I guess Alanna set down just under the first dray. I heard her cry out, just for a moment, and then stop. I grabbed my gun and came out and saw two of them carrying her off into the trees."

"They had two horses hidden inside the trees," the general said. "I heard them galloping away when I reached here."

Fargo's eyes were narrowed as he scanned the dark bulk of the trees. Harry had been more clever than he'd expected, Fargo muttered inwardly. He'd waited from on high and watched the camp begin to bed down until the darkness cloaked his view. But he'd seen enough and decided stealth was smarter than wild charges.

"We've got to go after them," the general demanded.

"No way, not in the dark," Fargo said.

"Come morning. We'll go after them, come morning. You can pick up the trail, Fargo," Taylor said.

"They'd like that, us charging right into their den," Fargo snorted.

"What's your idea then, for God's sake?" the general exclaimed.

"We wait. It won't be long before we hear from them," Fargo said. "He took Alanna as a bargaining chip."

"He's not getting my wagons," the general barked.

"Your wagons. Your daughter. Your decision," Fargo said. "I'd sleep real hard on it if I were you." He turned away and slowly retraced his steps to where he'd left his bedroll and clothes.

Elsa and Eva were still there and they watched him with wide-eyed apprehension.

"We have to get back," Elsa said. "The shots surely woke up Sally."

"She'll be mad when she finds we're not there," Eva put in.

"Or jealous, maybe," Fargo said, and they both shrugged uncertainly. "Tell her they took the general's daughter. That'll give her something to think about besides you."

"My gosh, is that what happened?" Elsa asked. "We'll sure tell her." They turned and hurried away together, and Fargo gathered his things and walked back to the campsite. He settled in beneath one of the drays and slept until the dawn woke him. He used his canteen to wash, and when he finished, he saw Morton Taylor leaning against the nearest wagon, deep lines of sleeplessness etched into his face.

"We just wait?" the general asked.

"That's right. It won't be long," Fargo said grimly. He took the tin mug of coffee offered to him and had just drained the last of it when his prediction was fulfilled as two horsemen appeared. Fargo spied the yellow kerchief on the one at the right and straightened as the two riders drew to a halt.

Harry speared the general with a deep, meaningful stare. "The wagons, Taylor," he growled.

"There's nothing but oil shale in the wagons," the general said, and licked his dry lips.

"No wagons, no daughter," Harry spat.

Fargo watched Morton Taylor swallow hard, his face churning with emotions. "All right, all right," the man muttered hoarsely.

"Smart," Harry grunted. "I'll send my men for them."

Fargo's thoughts raced against time. The man was the kind who'd erupt out of vicious anger if he didn't find anything. He'd shoot Alanna in sheer fury and frustration. "Not so fast," Fargo said as Harry started to turn away. The man's eyes grew narrow as he stared back.

"That voice," he murmured. "You're the joker who likes to shoot hats off."

"Or heads. Depends on my mood," Fargo said. "You bring the girl and look at the wagons here."

The man's eyes stayed narrowed. "You heard me. No wagons, no daughter."

"No daughter, no wagons," Fargo returned, and met the man's eyes with an unflinching stare.

Harry slowly turned his horse and rode away, his companion at his side.

"Good God, Fargo, you're playing with Alanna's life," Morton Taylor said.

"I'm trying to make sure she stays alive," Fargo answered.

"By challenging him?"

"By counting on one thing, greed. He wants those wagons more than anything else. He'll be back with her," Fargo said.

"And then?" the general asked.

"You give him the damn wagons. He won't give up Alanna till he's finished with them."

"He won't find anything more than the army did," the general said, but his voice was filled with nervousness.

"What happens then?"

"Real trouble, but we'll have a chance this way," Fargo said, and his glance went to Burt Roscoe. "Position your men at the edge of the trees. Harry will have to have his boys out in the open to examine the wagons. If it all breaks loose, we'll have the first advantage."

Roscoe nodded and immediately set about strategically placing the men in the treeline. He had just finished when the band of horsemen appeared, only eight now, Fargo noted in satisfaction. One of the men held

Alanna in the saddle in front of him and he rode along-side Harry. Fargo cast a quick glance at Roscoe's men in the trees. They were difficult to spot, he was glad to see. Harry reined up and dismounted, and the man holding Alanna slid from his horse and pulled her with him. Fargo saw he was holding a Remington Beals five-shot revolver against her stomach. If she were afraid, she was hiding it well, Fargo observed as she glared at the man holding her.

"One wrong move and the little lady gets her guts blown out," Harry warned, and his glance took in the general, Burt Roscoe, and Fargo.

"Yes, yes, no one's going to do anything," Taylor said. "But there's nothing in the wagons but shale, I tell you."

Harry motioned to the man holding Alanna and the heavy-set figure pulled her to one side. The gun stayed hard against her side as the man positioned himself half-behind her.

"Start with the first dray," Harry ordered, and he walked to the nearest wagon while his men dismounted. "Get the tarp off first," he said, and Fargo watched the men work with swift sureness. When the tarpaulin was off and flung aside, Harry joined with the rest of his men as they put their shoulder low against the bottom edge of the wagon. They lifted and pushed hard and the heavy wagon tipped and some of the shale spilled out. Finally the wagon fell on its side to spew the remainder of its cargo across the ground. Fargo saw the general wince, but Harry and his men were quickly kicking, pawing, and sorting through the shale. When it was obvious there was nothing hidden in or under the rocks, Harry kicked a hole in the floor-boards and cursed when he found nothing there.

"The next one," he snapped, and once again they lifted a big dray enough to spill some of its load out and then pushed it onto its side. It lay there, like the first wagon, with one set of its wheels spinning idly.

Harry and his men sorted through the shale again, and when he finished, he kicked in the floor of the wagon. But nothing was different from the first wagon and Fargo saw the man's jaw grow tighter.

They proceeded to the third wagon with the same results and Fargo shot a glance beyond where Sally, Elsa, and Eva patiently watched and waited. The fourth wagon yielded nothing and Harry turned on the general with a snarl. He reached one hand out and seized the man by the shirt front. "Where's the goddamn money?" he roared.

"There's no money. You heard wrong," Morton Taylor shouted back.

"The hell I did," the man cursed, and flung the general away from him.

"Where'd you hear the general was carrying money?" Fargo asked, his curiosity prompting the question.

"I got friends workin' for the army at Fort Morgan," Harry snarled. "Friends who get to see dispatches. Dispatches that said he's bringing a lot of money down to New Mexico."

"The dispatch was wrong, planted on purpose," the general snapped back. "You followed a bad lead."

Fargo saw Harry's gaze go past the general to where Sally sat atop the driver's seat of the Conestoga. His eyes narrowing again, he slowly turned back to Morton Taylor, an icy smile sliding across his face. "And maybe we've just been looking in the wrong place," Harry said. "Maybe you've been real smart, General. Maybe you figured that's just what everybody would do, look in your wagons when you've got it all hidden on those two over there."

"They've nothing to do with me," Morton Taylor said.

"Go get them," Harry ordered his men, and three riders hurried off to fetch Sally and the two wagons.

"Get off," Harry barked when the wagons were brought to him.

Eva and Elsa climbed down first, Sally taking her time to step from the Conestoga. "What do you want with us?" she yelled at Harry.

"Shut up and get over there," Harry ordered. He snapped commands to his men. "Take those damn wagons apart."

Two teams clambered into the wagons. They began to throw everything out of the two wagons—dresses, hatboxes, clothing bags, shoes, extra water flasks, a small chest that turned out to hold combs, jewelry, earrings, powder, and cologne bottles.

Fargo saw Harry's jaw begin to throb as more boxes full of similar objects were tossed from the wagons. Carefully, with casual slowness, Fargo began to ease his way backward and then sideways as more cartons and boxes were thrown from both wagons. He worked his way behind the man holding Alanna while everyone else's attention was riveted on the things being tossed out of the wagons. The heavy-set man's attention was also on the scene in front of him, and though he still held a gun on Alanna, its barrel no longer dug into her ribs.

"Nothing else in here," someone shouted from the Conestoga. "We took up the floorboards. Nothing under them, either. Same with the side panels."

"Nothing in here, either," someone else called from the Owensboro. Fargo eased forward, taking another step closer to the man holding Alanna.

Harry whirled on the general. "Where's the goddamn money?" he shouted.

"There is none, I told you," Morton Taylor shot back.

Fargo saw Harry's face twitch in barely controlled fury, and with one long, silent step, he came up behind the man holding Alanna. The Colt in his hand,

he pressed the barrel against the man's head just behind his ear.

"Drop the gun or I'll blow your brains from here to
the Rio Grande," he whispered. The hammer clicked
softly as he pulled it back and he felt the man's arm
relax as he dropped the gun from Alanna's side.

"Kill the bastards, all of 'em," Harry shouted.

Fargo's arm flashed out and closed around Alanna's
waist as he dived forward and flung her to the ground
just before the fusillade of gunfire erupted. He rolled
with her, came up behind a mound of shale, and saw
that gunfire from the trees was taking its toll. Harry's
men tried to take cover in the open, but he saw at least
four go down. The general had managed to fall behind
one of the overturned wagons and lay prone as bullets
smashed into the wood.

Fargo glimpsed two of Harry's men climbing onto
their horses and, clinging low to the saddle, racing
away. He caught motion to his left and saw a third
man run toward the horses, stumble, and dodge bullets
that plowed into the ground near him. A flash to his
right made Fargo spin, and he glimpsed the yellow
kerchief as Harry darted from one mound of shale to
the other until he was near one of the horses. The
Trailsman rose and waited for the man to come into
the open when he darted the dozen feet to the horse.
He raised the Colt as Harry came into view, rolling
along the ground, but suddenly Harry fired a barrage
of shots that were no less deadly for their wildness.
Fargo dropped as the hail of bullets whistled past his
head, some slamming into the shale. When he lifted
his head again, he saw Harry was on the horse, racing
away and pressed almost prone on the saddle. Fargo
straightened up and pulled Alanna to her feet.

Her black eyes were round and deep as she stared
at him. "Thank you. I'm grateful," she murmured.

"I'm glad it worked out as well as it did," Fargo

said, and turned to find Burt Roscoe nearby. "You lose anyone?" he asked.

"Two men," Roscoe answered. "It could've been a lot worse."

Morton Taylor came toward Roscoe, brushing dirt from himself. "Bury the men properly first," he said. "Then get the sack of tenpenny nails from the pack-horse. We need to fix those floorboards before we load up again."

Loading the four drays would take all day, Fargo realized. He started to wheel the pinto around.

"Where are you going?" Taylor asked.

"To see if I'm a good judge or character."

"What in hell does that mean?" the general barked.

"Harry's not the kind to just hightail it," Fargo said. "His kind needs revenge and he'll come back for it, even if it's just to kill one person. I'm not going to sit and wait and let him pick his moment." He sent the pinto into a gallop, crossed the level land, and picked up the trail of the four riders that had fled. Their hoof-prints stayed in groups of two, one and one, until they began to join together. Harry had been the last to flee and the prints of his horse stayed at the outside when he pulled up with the others. They had swung onto a slope, went through spruce and serviceberry, and slowed their pace.

Fargo slowed also and came to a stream where they'd stopped to let the horses drink. He picked up their tracks on the opposite bank and saw they had slowed to a steady trot with no thought that they were being followed. They came to a halt again, he determined as he reined to a stop. They'd dismounted and he read their footprints pressed into the soft soil, prints that crossed back and forth. Fargo let a hard smile touch his lips. They hadn't halted to rest but to argue, he deduced, and his glance moved up beyond the spot. Three of the horses had finally gone on, he saw, and the fourth went off to the right alone. That'd be Harry,

104

Fargo grunted, and he sent the pinto after the lone set of hoofprints. Unable to convince the others to go back with him, he'd left them to go their way while he rode off to have his revenge.

The man had made a wide circle, Fargo noted, then doubled back toward where the wagons had been camped. Harry hadn't hurried any and the sun had gone into the afternoon sky when Fargo began to close in on his quarry. He slowed again when he saw Harry had dismounted, his footprints clear in the soft soil as he led his horse by the reins.

Fargo swung to the ground and moved on silently while the Ovaro followed. But when he heard a twig snap as the Ovaro stepped on it, he halted, took the horse's reins, and dropped them over a low branch. He went forward alone, caution in the frown that creased his brow. He'd gone perhaps another few hundred yards when he heard the sound of a horse snorting in air. He went into a crouch and moved forward until he saw the horse. He dropped low and ducked behind a forest stand of rhododendron, crept forward, and finally spotted the figure crouched low behind a rock.

Harry had taken up a spot that let him cover the road just below where he expected the wagons would come along. Fargo dropped to one knee and unholstered the big Colt. Maybe he could get a few more details from the man about his source of information, Fargo mused as he raised his voice calmly, almost soothingly. "Stay right there, cousin," he said, and saw the man's figure stiffen in surprise. "You're a slow learner, aren't you, Harry?" Fargo remarked.

Harry pushed his hands against the rock and carefully turned around. "Bastard," he muttered.

"You do exactly what I say and I might just let you ride away from here in one piece," Fargo said. "First tell me about your friends that get to see U.S. Army dispatches." The man glowered and stared in stony silence and Fargo pulled the hammer back on the Colt. "You've got three seconds to talk," he said.

Harry used up two of the seconds before he broke the silence. "A trooper in the quartermaster's corp," he said. "He owes me a few and he passes things onto me."

"What exactly did he tell you he saw?" Fargo pressed.

"A dispatch to intercept the general's wagons because of information he was carrying a lot of money into New Mexico," Harry answered.

"Did it say why he was carrying it into New Mexico?"

"No," Harry said. "Just that they had advice he was carrying it."

Fargo turned the reply in his mind. It didn't add anything much to the picture, he grunted silently. But there was no reason for the army to concern itself over a man carrying money into New Mexico. That was private business . . . unless—and he paused in thought—they expected he was bringing it in to do something against the interests of official American policy. The thought plainly gave support to Alanna's story, Fargo frowned, only it was equally plain that the wagons carried no money and that fit the general's explanation of a false rumor purposely planted to stop him. Fargo grimaced. Once again, the answers refused to completely satisfy him, and he shook aside further speculation.

"Drop your gun belt, real careful and slow," Fargo ordered, and Harry obeyed. "Take your shirt off," Skye said and again the man obeyed, "and throw it over here." Fargo scooped the shirt up as it landed in front of him. He shook it out and no hidden pistols fell out. "Turn around," he ordered, and Harry slowly turned. No extra pocket pistols protruded from his belt, neither in front nor in back, and the Trailsman stepped forward, kicked the gun belt on the ground to

106

one side, and bent down to take the gun from the holster. He emptied cartridges from the chamber and flung gun and bullets far into the brush. Taking a step back, he met Harry's angry but apprehensive stare. "I'm going to be kind to you," Fargo said. "Start riding and keep riding."

He turned away from the man and his glance caught on the brown gelding. The horse had shifted position and Fargo saw the rifle holster on the other side of the saddle. It hung empty, and the instant of realization exploded inside him just as he heard the darting movement behind him. His curse froze in his throat and he flung himself forward in a headlong dive just as the shot exploded. He felt the bullet graze the top of his temple as he hit the ground, and an array of yellow and red flashes erupted inside his head. He managed to roll and the flashes snapped off, but another shot smashed a tree trunk inches from his head and he rolled again. Harry was racing at him, firing again but too quickly, and the third shot was wide. Fargo tried to bring his arm around to fire, but the man was on top of him, bringing the rifle barrel down to fire point-blank. Fargo dropped his own gun, dug his hands into the soft earth for support, and kicked out with one leg. It caught Harry hard in the knee just as he fired again and Fargo felt the warmth of the bullet that grazed his ear. The man was off-balance for an instant, enough time for Fargo to close his hands around the barrel of the rifle and twist as he flung his body sideways. Harry hung on but went down on his knees and Fargo kicked backward and felt his heel slam into the man's jaw. Harry's grip on the rifle stock fell away as he went backward and Fargo spun, leaping to his feet in time to see Harry half-diving, half-slithering across the ground to where the Colt lay.

With a curse, Fargo sprang and brought the rifle down with both hands in a tremendous smash that caught the man across the back of the neck. Harry gave a strange, choking-coughing sound that covered the snap of his neck vertebrae. He half-rose on his hands and knees, gave another gasp of the strange sound, and fell forward to lay silently. Ever so slowly, a trickle of blood appeared at one corner of his mouth and Fargo straightened up and dropped the gun on the ground. Mistakes, he grunted bitterly, they always came up to make you sorry.

He hadn't noticed the empty rifle holster on the far side of the horse and the man had placed the gun on the ground alongside the rock where it lay out of sight. He drew a deep breath as he walked away. He'd been willing to let the man ride away and had almost lost his life for it. But he was the one walking away, he reflected. Maybe it was his reward for a gesture in the right direction.

He reached the Ovaro, mounted, and let the horse slowly make its way through the fast-gathering dusk. His gaze swept the high hills on both sides and he glimpsed a trio of silent horsemen as they faded into the high spruce. Some tribes would sit back and wait to see if the white men killed one another off but the Apache would see it all as a gross intrusion on their territory, sort of like unwanted outsiders picnicking in one's backyard. He rode on grimly, and when he reached the wagons, there was still a little light left. The four drays had been turned back upright and the men were just putting the tarpaulins on again.

Fargo frowned as he looked past the drays to see that the Conestoga and the Owensboro were a hundred yards back again. "What are they doing back there?" he asked.

"I told them to get away from here," the general said. "What happened didn't change anything about that. I don't want anyone near my wagons."

"What the hell do you think they're going to do to your damn shale?" Fargo snapped.

"I don't care. I'm not having anybody with my wagons. I'm having enough trouble now. I'm taking no chances," Morton Taylor said.

Fargo's eyes were narrowed as he turned away. The man's stand didn't make sense. Three girls weren't about to hurt his shale. He was running on a gigantic sense of mistrust and fear, and the events that had happened made him seem justified on that. But his unreasonableness about Sally and the other two girls said more than that. It said that there was something more he was afraid of, Fargo pondered, maybe something the army and the bandits had missed. But what? Fargo grimaced at himself. Why was he so damned bothered about wagons that were plainly not carrying anything? It made no sense. He grunted and put aside further thoughts as Alanna approached.

"I'm sorry," she said. "He's a very stubborn man."

"This is his last night for it," Fargo growled, and she didn't press him to add to his answer.

"You still won't believe me?" Alanna asked.

"There's still no proof of it. But I'm wondering more," he allowed.

"I guess I should be grateful for small favors."

"Yep."

"You'll come apologizing to me yet," she said.

"Maybe."

She gestured with a nod toward Sally's distant wagons. "You going down there for the night?" she asked.

"Close enough. Unless you've any better ideas."

"I don't," she said stiffly, and strode away. He watched her walk into the darkness, narrow hips held in tight, yet a definite sway to her movements. He turned and took the Ovaro by the reins and led the horse across the grass toward Sally's wagons. He halted near the edge of the trees when he reached the halfway point, and set out his things. He was almost undressed when he spotted the lone figure moving toward him from the Conestoga. He watched as Sally Jamison halted beside him. Her small nose, pert face, and short brown hair outlined under a pale moon, her small figure wrapped in a light blue silk robe, she seemed both very determined and very small.

"Came to talk about Elsa and Eva visiting you," she said. "They told me they wanted to thank you for helping us up the high slope with the wagons."

Fargo smiled inwardly. The two girls hadn't mentioned the first visit. "Something wrong with that?" Fargo inquired, and watched her eyes take in the smooth muscled form of his chest and shoulders.

"No, except they know I decide about thanking around here," Sally said.

"Maybe they're tired of that," Fargo offered affably, and saw the light-brown eyes narrow.

"They can live with it awhile longer," Sally said.

"You come to do the thanking?" Fargo asked.

"Maybe," she said, and lowered herself to the edge of the bedroll. "But I came asking, too," she said.

"That's honest enough." he commented.

"I'm afraid hanging so far back with the Apache all around," she said. "I want to be up with the general's wagons."

"No threats this time? Just asking?" Fargo slid at her.

"Guess so," Sally answered gravely.

"I'd figured on seeing to that tomorrow night," Fargo told her. "Honesty deserves honesty."

"And a good deed deserves a good deed," she said, she leaned forward, her lips pressing onto his mouth. Firm lips, a little thin, but there was a directness to the kiss and he felt her tongue slip out for just an instant and draw back at once. His hand went to the neck of the robe and slid down the edge of the fabric; the robe parted to reveal smallish breasts, neatly curved at the bottoms, brown-pink areola surrounding nipples of the same shade that were larger than he'd expected on the somewhat flat breasts. Her hand moved, pulling the remainder of the robe open, and

110

she lay back, a small, neat body with protruding hip-bones, a flat belly, and a modestly curly triangle under it. Her legs just avoided thinness but held their own shapeliness.

She shrugged the robe from her entirely and her arms came around his neck, pulling him down to her, and her mouth opened, reaching hungrily for him, and this time her tongue was a seeking, sliding, slipping invitation. He felt her hands slide down his last piece of clothing and clutch at the firmness of his buttocks, She gasped in pleasure at the tough muscle. He bent his face down, took one smallish breast into his mouth and pulled at it. "Ah, good God, aaahhh," Sally breathed, pressing herself upward to push all of her breast into his mouth. "Aaaaooooh," she breathed again, a happy sigh, then she pulled back and offered the other breast. He felt her thinnish legs lift, fall open, and come together around one of his oaken thighs and her body twisted to rub her flat belly and the curly nap below it against his organ. "Ah, jeeez . . . ah, ah, yes, oh, God, yes," Sally gasped, and one arm half around her small waist, he turned her on her back. Her legs drew upward instantly, knees pulled high, almost as though she were going to leap upward and forward.

"Open, oh, it's opened for you, Fargo . . . look, look, take . . ," Sally murmured, and her position indeed offered the portal to pleasure opened wide. He saw her quiver and her pelvis trembled and he slid across and through, bringing his own stiffened desire up against her. She gave a high-pitched cry, almost a squeak and pushed up to close the soft, liquid lips around him. He took a moment to thrill to the tender heat that touched him. He slid forward to find her sur-prisingly wide, and her knees came down, legs clasp-ing him around the buttocks. "Harder, Fargo," Sally Jamison murmured between cries of pleasure. "Oh, jeeez, harder." He obeyed and heard her cry out at once. "Yes, oh, yes, that's it . . . oh, yes," she said, and she surprised him with the strength of her answering thrusts. "Ah, eeeee . . . ah, ah, eeee . . ." Sally uttered, varying tiny gasps with long cries, and the small breasts quivered against him as her arms locked around his neck. Her climax was sudden, sooner than he'd expected, and he heard the note of almost panic in her voice. "Now, oh, jeeez, now, now . . . harder, harder, oh . . . aaaggggh," Sally cried out, her gasped words ending in a gargling kind of cry that stayed half in her throat.

He felt her slam her pelvis against him and hold it there in a long, quivering moment as she lifted herself by her legs, feet pressed hard against the ground. A long, disappointed sigh slid from her lips finally and her legs came up to once again cross behind his back. He felt himself throbbing inside her, a sweetly warm sensation, and she made a tiny sound of disappointment when he finally left her and she stretched her legs out tightly. It had been pleasurable but there'd been none of the throbbing, overwhelming earthiness of Elsa and Eva. Sally Jamison had surprised him by her quickness which had bordered on the perfunctory, and she surprised him again as her eyes moved across his face and she sat up, the smallish breasts turning to him. "It's always like this with me the first time," she said. "I've got to get to know someone before I can really relax."

"You pick up quick on things." Fargo smiled.

She shrugged and didn't return the smile. "I feel it. You've got to feel it," she said as she reached out for the robe and slipped it on.

"Maybe," he conceded. "You telling me there'll be another time?"

"Maybe," she echoed, tossing him a tiny smile as she stood up. "Thanks for tomorrow," she said, and hurried away.

Fargo watched her small shape go through the night until she reached the Conestoga. A complex young woman, he decided. She'd first come on with hard-headed determination and obstinate fury; then she showed she could be waiflike and vulnerable; and now, when he'd least expected it, she revealed an edge of coldness. He turned on his side and went to sleep, grateful for the simplicity of slumber.

When morning came he took his things back to the general's wagons and found the man impatiently waiting. "We've lost an entire day. I hope we can make some of it up."

"In these mountains?" Fargo retorted. "Just hope you don't lose another day." He climbed onto the Ovaro and saw Alanna brushing her raven locks, standing in a white shirt and pink petticoat and radiating a warm but aristocratic beauty. He took a tin mug of coffee one of the men handed up to him, sipped it slowly, and enjoyed watching the way the long breasts lifted, swayed, and came down with each stroke of the hairbrush. She finished, her eyes passing over him with barely a nod.

He returned the empty mug and waved a hand at the wagons, and their drivers began to roll them forward. With a quick glance, he saw Sally, Eva, and Elsa begin to follow, and he rode on along a curving trail that grew narrower but allowed enough room for the wagons to squeeze through. It ended in a straight but steep dip downward into a gulley thick with hackberry.

Fargo rode on ahead after he waved the lead wagon forward. The gulley lasted for perhaps three miles to end at a spot where two paths converged. One was far too narrow and steep for the wagons; the other was a trail through the remains of a burned-out spruce forest where blackened trunks of once-proud trees stood like charred sentinels, guarding the new seedlings that were beginning to sprout. The path through was littered with the remains of burned and fallen trees, and the general's face filled with dismay as he rode to a halt.

"Impossible. We'd split our wheels, even if we

pulled aside logs every few feet," the man said. "You'll have to find another trail."

"Not without doubling back. You'll lose another day," Fargo said. "I think you can make it without splitting your wheels if you go real slow and only pull aside the big ones."

Morton Taylor eyed the passage and shook his head. "Too much of a risk. We'll double back."

Fargo shrugged as he scanned the passage through again. He was still convinced the wagons could make it with care, but he turned and rode back the way he'd come.

He finally reached the beginning of the gulley, surveyed the mountains to the north and west, and sent the pinto up a pass between two gnarled spruce. He found a trail, uneven and full of sharp twists but negotiable, and he followed it west where it continued on in a long, slow curve to finally point south. He spotted three other trails but found when he investigated that they all ended abruptly at the edge of ravines or mountain cliffs, and he slowly returned down to the entrance of the gulley.

He rode with his jaw set. He had seen more than mountain trails. Two sets of Mescalero had watched him from the high crags and he saw them finally converge to make their way into thick cedar stands.

He rode unhurried, but from under the brim of his hat his lake-blue eyes continued to scan the hills and he spied the leaves moving above him in a steady line. The Mescalero were not riding on. They were staying, edging down closer. But they were still only watching and Fargo knew they'd move with their usual caution. He reached the mouth of the gulley to find the four drays and, at least a hundred yards back, Sally and her wagons. He estimated there was another two hours of daylight left and he took the wagons onto the narrow and twisting trail that led west. The terrain was pitted and made of sudden, sharp dips, so traveling was slow.

When dusk descended, he led the wagons into a half-curve of thick spruce set back deep from the trail. "Line up against that end," Fargo said, gesturing. "That'll leave room for the Conestoga and the Owensboro over here."

"The hell it will," Morton Taylor snapped instantly.

"They come up with us from now on," Fargo said. "I told you, no other outfits with my wagons."

"What in hell are three girls going to do to your wagons?" Fargo demanded.

"I don't care. I'm not having them with us," the man insisted.

"You leave them back there and you'll be handing them to the Mescalero."

"Nonsense. If the Mescalero strike they'll hit us, too," the general said.

"Not necessarily. They're like a wolf pack. They'll go after stragglers first. Sally Jamison's bringing her wagons up here," Fargo told him.

"You're disobeying my orders. I won't allow that," Taylor shouted.

"I'm doing what I think's right. I won't allow anything else," Fargo said, and sent the Ovaro into a trot. He rode partway to the Conestoga and waved and Sally set the wagons rolling forward. He waited, rode back to the half-circle with her, and had her put her wagons into place. Eva and Elsa gave him big grins as they climbed down and Sally's smile had generous measure of satisfaction in it.

The general glared at the three young women. "Don't expect anything from me and stay out of my way," he growled.

Fargo saw Alanna come up to look on, her face a quiet mask. "I think you all best realize something," he said. "For better or for worse, we've got to stay together. Even then, we're in a lot of trouble. We've only ten guns left, including me and Alanna. Add Sally

115

here and her cousins and we have thirteen. I figure there'll be at least twenty Mescalero coming at us, maybe twenty-five. Unless I can figure some way to even those odds, this could be the end of the trail and right now I don't have any ideas at all." His eyes swept the group gathered before him and paused on Morton Taylor.

"Only till this is over," the man muttered.

"It'll be over when you reach Cimarron," Fargo said, and turned away. He unsaddled the pinto and took down his bedroll. He'd started past the Conestoga when Sally appeared from around the back with a bucket of water. "Happy, now?" he asked, and her smile still held the satisfaction in it."

"Yes," she admitted. "But you could've brought it about at the beginning."

"No, and I didn't bring it about," Fargo said. "The Mescalero did."

She thought about the reply for a moment and shrugged. "No matter," she said, and hurried into the wagon.

Elsa and Eva poked their heads from the Owensboro as he passed and threw him identically cheerful smiles.

"Where will you bed down?" Eva asked.

"Not far enough away tonight. Besides, I have to think things out," Fargo said, and they looked disappointed in unison. He laughed, walked on, found a spot where the curve of spruce began, and set down his things. He undressed, lay back, let his thoughts tumble freely. There'd be no talk about the wagons with the Mescalero, no overturnings and fruitless searchings. They'd have no interest in the wagons. The Apache wanted guns, clothes, watches, anything they could use for trade. But mostly they wanted the pleasure of killing those who dared to violate their territories. Unlike the Plains tribes, the battle itself was relatively unimportant to the Apache. Stories of bravery told around the long winter campfire meant little to the Mescalero. War was never a game with them but always an exercise in deadly reality where there were only winners and losers.

Fargo swore silently as tumbling thoughts brought no answers, and before he dropped off to sleep, he decided that the only option open to him was to try to find a place that'd give them a chance to hold off an attack.

He slept restlessly and was awake when the first gray of dawn appeared over the high crags. He dressed, led the Ovaro away from camp, and rode on along the curving trail, his eyes searching for a place to make a stand. He spotted two that were far from ideal but might have to do, and he grimaced at the number of narrow passages down from the high hills. The Mescalero could come down any number of them, and when he turned to go back to the campsite, he could see the edges of flat stone places up among the high crags and knew the Mescalero waited in one of them.

The others had finished their coffee when he reached the wagons, and he saw Elsa and Eva talking to Burt Roscoe, as bright and bubbly as if he'd never mentioned the Apache.

"Where've you been?" The general frowned.

"Trying to find a place that might keep us alive," Fargo said.

"You find one?" Alanna asked, stepping forward.

"None that makes me happy," he said. "Let's roll. Might as well make time while we can."

"I'll ride along with you," Alanna said, and got her horse and caught up to him as he went on ahead. "I'm glad you insisted the Jamison girl and her cousins stay with us," she said. "Father seems a man obsessed, afraid of everything."

"I noticed," Fargo said dryly.

"Do you think we've a chance to get through?" she asked.

"A chance," he said grimly as his gaze swept the

117

high land. He saw no horsemen come into sight and he passed the first of the two places that might let them make a stand. There was still no sign of the Mescalero when he reached the second, and his lips bit down onto each other as he paused. "Let's keep going," he announced, as much to himself as anyone else. "They're giving us time, for some reason. Let's make the most of it." He moved the wagons forward, knowing he was taking a calculated risk, but neither of the two places had been ideal. He put the Ovaro into a canter and Alanna followed. Again he spied a place that would let them make a stand but left more than a little to be desired. He rode on as the sun passed the noon sky and finally halted where a fair-sized stream coursed across the curving path. He dismounted, his gaze sweeping the quiet hills, and he let the Ovaro drink. He knelt down at the stream, refilled his canteen, and found Alanna beside him.

"I've something to say," she remarked, the black eyes grave. "Except I can't seem to get the words right."

"Stop trying to get them right," Fargo told her. "Just spit it out."

"I'm sorry I couldn't stop you back in Claysville," she said. "I hate you for bringing him this far, but I'm very grateful to you for everything you've done on the trail. That doesn't make sense, does it?"

"It does, in its own way."

"And I'm grateful for what you did for me. I'd be dead now if it weren't for you," she said. Her hand came out and closed around his. "I'm sorry we couldn't have met differently. I think I'd have liked that."

"You might still like it," Fargo said, and he reached forward, pulled her to him, and let his mouth close down on her lips. They were soft lips, firm yet sweet, and she held back and then let herself respond for a moment, her tongue moving to touch his lips, and then she pulled away. She stood up quickly, her longish breasts swaying as she half-whirled.

"No," she breathed. "You have your own kind of integrity, Fargo. I have mine. I won't bargain with you that way."

"Don't see anything so fancy as integrity in it," Fargo said. "Just plain, old-fashioned wanting."

Alanna met his eyes, and the edge of a smile touched her lips. "I'll have to think about that," she said, and moved away as the first dray rolled to a halt.

Fargo let the horses drink and Sally lined her wagons up alongside the others. "We keep moving," he said. "They're holding back. We've nothing to lose by moving on."

"You find a place to stand yet?" the general asked.

"No," Fargo said, and sent the Ovaro into a canter. He scanned the high crags as he rode, and felt the uneasiness circling inside him. The Mescalero were waiting and that meant they'd something different in mind. He kept the pinto at a fast canter but slowed when he rounded a sharp twist in the trail. Lightning had hit hard at the spot some months back and three big cedars had been splintered and thrown into a pile of jagged, huge shards that stuck into the air at an assortment of angles. They formed a spikelike barrier with just enough room to bring the wagons around to the other side, he saw, and he nodded with grim satisfaction. It was probably as good a place to make a stand as any.

He waited for the others to arrive. When they did, he placed each wagon behind the spiked barricades with the help of Burt Roscoe, and when the task was finished, he estimated there were still a few hours of daylight left.

"Why haven't they come at us yet?" the general asked.

Damned if I know," Fargo said. "When you find out, you can be sure you won't like it." He glanced

119

to one side, then the other. Everyone waited in place, the women spaced in between the men along the line of wagons. There were only two passages down from the high land near the place. The Mescalero would have to come at them head on and leap the jagged barricade of splintered trees. They'd be open targets, unable to twist or turn. It might just be enough to even the odds, Fargo murmured silently. Only the Mescalero seldom did the expected, he added grimly. He snapped off idle wonderings when he caught the trickle of loose stones tumbling down the nearest passage. "Heads down," Fargo called out, and a moment later the Mescalero came into sight, moving single-file down the path. But there was no galloping charge as the line of partly naked riders emerged from the passage and slowly spread out.

"There are only ten of them," the general said.

"Only ten they want you to see for now," Fargo muttered, and his eyes were on the Mescalero in the center sitting atop a brown-and-white pony. The Indian wore a tattered army kerchief around his waist that made a statement of its own. Slowly, the Apache rode toward the log barricade, the others staying behind. A few held carbines, Fargo noted, the rest short, powerful bows. The Indian came to a halt a few feet from the logs, and Fargo saw his small, glittering black eyes take in the defense.

Rising to his feet, Fargo stepped forward and drew the Indian's contemptuous stare. The Apache had their own tongue and Fargo knew only a few words in it but many times they spoke Shoshonean because it was more widely used. The Indian spoke in short, curt phrases and Fargo was glad to hear the language he knew better.

"We take woman. You go free," the Indian said. Fargo smiled inwardly as he turned and let his eyes move across the four girls. Slowly, he returned his gaze to the Mescalero chief and waited. "That one," the Indian said, raised his arm, and pointed to Alanna.

Fargo heard Morton Taylor start to sputter. "Shut up," he snapped tersely, and the general fell silent. Fargo motioned to Alanna, and her eyes wide and round with apprehension, she came around the wagon and ducked under the splintered logs to halt beside him. Fargo let the Apache take her in and watched the man's eyes devour her. When he had allowed enough time, he motioned for Alanna to return behind the barricade and faced the Apache chief. He extended his palm and jingled imaginary coins in it.

The Indian shook his head. "You go free," he repeated. It was his price, Fargo knew, and a damn lie to boot. But the motions had been made and now he touched his temple with one finger.

The Apache's imperturbable expression remained, but the small black eyes took on an added glitter. "How long?" he questioned in Shoshonean.

Fargo used sign language for morning and the Indian thought for a moment, then slowly turned his pony and rode away. The others fell in silently behind him and filed out of sight into the narrow passage. Fargo waited a moment more and returned to the others beside the wagons.

"Why didn't you just tell him no?" the general barked. "Why all that back-and-forth rubbish?"

"I wanted to buy time," Fargo said. "And I wanted him to think we'd talk over the offer. He'll wait till morning now. Only I won't."

"Meaning what?" Alanna asked.

Fargo strode to the Ovaro and pulled himself onto the horse. "They'll come attacking in the morning, but without their chief it won't be the same."

"You'll never do it, man," Burt Roscoe said.

"I'm going to try," Fargo answered. "We'll need something more than the barricades. Maybe this will do it."

"What if you don't come back?" Alanna asked.

"Shoot carefully. Wait till they're jumping the barricades." Fargo smiled, wheeled the pinto around, and rode away in the falling dusk. He entered the narrow passageway the Mescalero had taken, slowed the horse to a walk as it quickly grew steep, and neared the top of the twisting crevice as dusk turned to night. He halted, swung to the ground, and proceeded the last few hundred yards on foot. The passage opened onto a rocky ledge, mostly flat with a sprinkling of mountain dwarf maple. The Apache camp lay directly in front of him, a small fire in the center. They were so confident they hadn't posted a single sentry.

Fargo tethered the Ovaro just inside the entrance to the passage and flattened himself against the ground. He crept forward, scanned the Indians in their loose circle around the fire, and counted at least twenty. He swore silently and crept forward again, his eyes moving across the party of braves spread out from the small fire. Finally he spotted the army kerchief on a figure behind the fire, and he watched the Indians begin to settle down for the night. The chief stayed where he was, and Fargo swore again. He had hoped the chief might go off by himself, but it wasn't to be. The chief started to stretch out plumb in the center of his braves and Fargo stayed flattened on the ground, his lips a thin and unhappy line.

He waited and watched the Mescalero settle down to sleep. A few took a ridiculously long time but they finally dropped off into a hard-breathing, snorting slumber. Slowly, Fargo began to crawl forward on his belly until he reached one of the dwarf maples. The large bushy tree was only a few dozen feet from the nearest of the sleeping Apache and gave him a clear view of where the chief lay near the fire, still surrounded on both sides by slumbering warriors. Fargo settled back against the tree and made plans for the morning.

He wouldn't use the Colt, he'd already decided. Split seconds would count and he'd estimated he'd need thirty seconds to reach the mouth of the passage and another five to get to the Ovaro. That was cutting it close, but with luck he could do it. Surprise would give him from five to ten seconds, he guessed. He'd use up three doing the thing he came to do and five to ten more starting his race for the passageway. All of which meant he needed the extra precious time that would come from awareness slowly turning to comprehension. A sharp, sudden shot would erase those extra moments, and that meant the throwing knife in the holster around his calf.

He settled back, certain of what he'd have to do, knowing there'd be no room for a miss or a mistake. Closing his eyes, he dozed the night away as he waited for morning when his life would be measured in only a few seconds.

7

He was awake when the first gray tint slid across the
sky but the Mescalero only began to stir as the sun
creeped over the high peaks. Three braves near him
woke, stretched, and began to sit up but Fargo's gaze
went past the figures to focus on the chief just beyond
the burned-out fire. As he watched, he saw the man
stir, sit up, and slowly begin to push himself to his
feet. Fargo's hand slid to the holster at his calf and he
drew a slender, double-edged throwing knife often
called an ''Arkansas toothpick.'' He measured the distance to the Apache chief—some twenty feet, he decided—drew his arm back and waited a moment more
as the three nearest Apache turned away. The Mescalero chief stood alone for an instant, one hand on the
stolen army kerchief he wore. With all the strength of
his powerful shoulder muscles, Fargo sent the blade
hurtling through the thin, morning air.

He was racing from beside the bushy tree even before the knife buried itself into the Apache's chest. Out
of the corner of his eye he saw the man stagger and
seize the hilt of the blade with both hands as, his mouth
open, he made soundless gasps and sank to the ground.
Fargo drove his powerful legs forward as he streaked
for the passageway and heard the sudden shouts of
alarm. They had seen him first and he glanced back to
see a half-dozen Mescalero hesitate, turning their gaze
from him to their chief on the ground. These were the
precious seconds he'd counted on, Fargo reminded

himself as he raced to the passage. He saw the Mescalero gather themselves and direct their fury toward his flying figure, but he was already into the passageway, the Ovaro waiting a dozen yards below. Their shouts filled the air with wild fury and he heard the sound of their ponies starting to race after him. He vaulted onto the Ovaro and had the horse into a full gallop in seconds, careening down the narrow passageway, taking twisting curves with reckless abandon. The sound of the pursuing Mescalero reverberated down the passage and he winced in pain as his right leg struck against a protruding rock at one of the sharp turns, but he kept the pinto racing full out.

The end of the passage came into sight and Fargo charged into the open, yanked the pinto around, and raced for the wagons and the barricade. He steered for the lowest of the barriers and glimpsed Burt Roscoe standing, two of the other men with him, a mixture of amazement and relief on their faces. The pinto landed nicely and Fargo leapt from the horse, yanking the Sharps from the saddle holster. He whirled as his feet hit the ground and he saw the first line of Mescalero trying to leap the barricades. Four cleared the splintered logs and a fusillade of gunfire erupted from the wagons and the four riders toppled from their horses. Two of the short-legged Indian ponies failed to clear the spiked logs and screamed in pain as their hides were torn open. Their riders were flung into the air and Fargo followed one with the rifle, firing as the man hit the ground, and the Apache stayed where he'd fallen.

The others were coming hard, some leaping the natural barriers, others trying to go around the ends, and another few slamming into the sharp points. Fargo brought down two more of the Apache who managed to get through and he saw the steady gunfire from the wagons was hitting hard at the attackers. But still another wave came up with shrieking shouts, and this time they split into two groups that leapt over the ends of the barriers as a third band came head-on. Fargo brought one down with a shot that smashed the Indian's chest in, and he spun as he heard Alanna's voice, a sharp, gasped cry. She tried to twist away from a Mescalero that had leapt at her from his mount while she had been trying to reload the rifle in her hand. The Indian grasped her by her raven hair and yanked and she went down with a scream of pain. He was atop her instantly, trying to hold her down as she twisted and clawed at him.

Their flailing arms hit at each other and Alanna tried to roll but the Apache pressed his weight down on her. A shot would be too risky, Fargo swore, and he leapt forward, turning the big Sharps in his hands as the Apache brought one arm up, a jagged-edged bone hunting knife in his hand. Fargo swung the stock of the rifle, reaching out with his long arms, and the blow caught the Indian across the forehead, the man's head snapping back as he fell to one side. Fargo rushed forward and smashed the heavy rifle stock down again, driving it into the Apache's throat with all his weight behind it. The Indian gave a gargling sound as his esophagus collapsed and a small fountain of red cascaded from his mouth.

Fargo started to pull Alanna to her feet when he caught the sudden shadow and he flung himself forward half over the young woman. The Mescalero swept past, leaning far out from his pinto, and swiped with a tomahawk. The blow grazed Fargo's hat. As he raced by, the Apache tried to pull up his pony too sharply. The horse lost footing and went down and its rider flew off, hit the ground, and came up with his tomahawk raised. He let out a whooping scream and charged and Fargo's shot slammed almost point-blank into the man's waist. The Apache doubled almost in two and fell to the ground.

Fargo looked up as the gunfire stopped and he saw

126

the rest of the Mescalero fleeing back into the narrow passage. He rose, pulling Alanna with him, and she leaned against him for a few moments. When she stepped back, her black eyes stayed on him.

"Jesus," Fargo heard Burt Roscoe breathe in awe and relief. "I thought we were goners. How could it have been worse with their chief along?"

"Control, direction, and spirit," Fargo said. "They attacked wildly and lost too many. Now they'll hightail it to make camp and choose another chief. That'll take at least a week." He swept the littered ground with a quick glance. "We lose anybody?" he asked.

"Trainor," the foreman said.

"Bury him, and let's get out of here."

As Burt Roscoe and the rest of his men set to their task, Fargo found a small rainwater pool and let the Ovaro drink. Sally, Elsa, and Eva sat their wagons patiently, he saw, and when he returned to the barricades, the others were ready to move on.

"We going to have more trouble with those damn savages?" the general muttered.

"Not those, but there are plenty of others in these mountains," Fargo said, and started the Ovaro forward. He heard the sound of hooves following and saw Alanna hurrying after him.

"May I ride along?" she asked, and he let his brows lift.

"May I?" he echoed. "You turning over a new leaf?"

Her smile was wry. "I guess I deserved that," she said. "Maybe I did everything wrong from the start, but I'd do it again. There didn't seem to be any other way and I haven't changed my mind on any of it. I still don't want him to go through with this."

"Confession time?" Fargo remarked.

"Maybe, but I really came to tell you that I'm afraid, Fargo, more afraid than when we started," she said, and drew a frown from the big man beside her. "We've

127

gotten through everything that's happened so far, mostly thanks to you. But this can't go on. His luck won't hold out forever.''

''It could, especially if he's been right all along about somebody planting rumors,'' Fargo said. ''Seems to me that everyone's taken a turn and come up empty-handed.''

''No rumors,'' Alanna said. ''No rumors.''

''You stick to your guns, I'll give you that,'' Fargo commented.

''I know what I heard at home. I just wish I could make you believe me,'' she said, and the arrogance in her voice had been replaced by an almost tearful resignation. ''It's all been for nothing.''

''What has?'' Fargo queried.

''You saving his life. It's like rescuing someone from death so they can be hung,'' Alanna said.

It was Fargo's turn for a wry smile. She had her own succinct way with words, he grunted. ''His wasn't the only life on the line,'' he reminded her.

''I know,'' she said, her black eyes round. ''We'll talk more later—tonight, maybe.'' She wheeled her horse around and set off in a canter to rejoin the wagons, her slender, straight back held tall in the saddle.

Fargo rode on, quickening his pace, and his gaze searched the high land until he came to where the trail began to turn back southward. The land suddenly became soft and sandy, sandstone pinnacles rising in sets of threes, and he 'let the Ovaro step carefully. The horse's feet sank in at once, almost up to the fetlock at one spot, and Fargo swung to the ground and felt himself go into the soft soil. His gaze narrowed as he walked the horse forward through the sandy terrain and he saw that the stretch of soil came to an end some hundred yards on and the ground grew firm again.

He reached the harder ground and saw mountain spruce bordering both sides of the trail. He dismounted and stared back along the sandy section: one of nature's unexpected bag of tricks, he grimaced, a stretch where for hundreds, maybe thousands of years the winds had blown against the sandstone pinnacles to carry tiny flecks of sand down onto the trail, day by day and night by night over the aeons, building the short stretch of shifting, sucking terrain. The teams could never pull the heavily laden drays across it, Fargo knew, and he swore silently. Certainly not with their own weight driving them down into the sand. They'd have all they could do just to pull themselves across. Dropping the pinto's reins over a low branch, he began to walk back across the Sand stretch. He stayed to the side where the footing was a trifle firmer, and when he reached the other end, he saw Morton Taylor leading the first dray, Alanna beside him.

Fargo waited till the others arrived before he spoke in short, terse sentences as the general stared at the stretch of land. "Unhitch two teams and walk them across," Fargo said. "They'll have tough-enough going as it is. When you're finished, go back and get the other two teams. We'll take Sally's wagons last."

Burt Roscoe quickly obeyed. Fargo accepted the compliment of no questions being asked. He watched from the side as the two teams struggled their way across the sand, burdened by their body weight and helped by the strength of their draft-horse blood. They finally reached the firm ground at the end and took in deep drafts of air while the next two teams began to make their laborious way across.

"Tie the reins together, then double the strands of lariat," Fargo said. "I figure between all of us we've enough lariat to reach." He joined with the others as they began to knot the double lariats to the reins until, Burt Roscoe at his side, he dragged the long ropes back across the sand and bound the ends securely to the first wagon. At his signal, the teams on the solid ground began to pull and Fargo apprehensively watched the first dray sink almost to its hubcaps in the sand. But the wheels slowly turned and he was grateful to see that the deep sand remained loosely packed.

The sun had begun to slide toward dusk when the Owensboro was finally pulled across and onto the firm ground. It took another hour to untangle and untie harnesses and lariats and wind all the ropes up and hitch the teams in place. Fargo was happy to find a large hollow of stone and cottonwoods only a half-hour on, and he waved the wagons in as the sun disappeared over the high peaks. The cook got a fire started and Fargo hungrily accepted the plate of beef jerky and hot beans. He had just finished and returned his plate when he saw the general slowly walk around each of his drays, carefully inspecting the wagons.

"You're right," Fargo said, and the general turned, startled. "No wagon's built for this kind of terrain. They could snap an axle or split a wheel at any time."

"I can't have that," Morton Taylor said, alarm instant in his voice. "These wagons must get to Cimarron. From now on you ride farther ahead. If a trail goes bad, you find another one. Time's not as important as getting there."

"Your choice," Fargo said. "I figure we're not more than a few days from the New Mexico border. We're also going into the Chiricahua Apache territory."

"Are they worse than the Mescalero?" the man asked.

"They're sure no better," Fargo said. "The faster we get out of these mountians, the happier I'll be."

"I'm not risking the wagons any more than I have to," the man insisted, and Fargo shrugged as he turned away. He passed Sally beside Elsa and Eva and all three girls showed tiredness in their faces.

"It's been a hard few days," Fargo said. "But I haven't noticed you doing much to find your folks."

"That's not so. We've searched every bit of land we

130

covered. We looked to see anything: broken wagon wheel, old trunks, anything," Sally protested.

"You'd have noticed if you'd been back with us," Eva concurred, and Elsa nodded.

"Maybe," Fargo said. "Still seems like trying to find a needle in a haystack."

"We just had to try," Sally said.

Fargo strolled on. He took his things from the Ovaro and went up a slope to the right to where a bed of spruce needles offered a soft carpet for his bedroll. He undressed to his drawers, placed the Colt beside him, and relaxed under the warm night blanket. The night sounds echoed; the soft whirr of insect wings, the clicking of stag beetles, the distant cry of a nighthawk, and the steady rustling of white-footed deer mice. He had closed his eyes when his wild-creature hearing picked up the sound of leaves being brushed aside. He rose on one elbow, his hand closing around the Colt, and listened to soft footsteps moving tentatively, unsurely up the slope.

He peered through the darkness where a weak moon allowed only a thin light and he spied the figure pushing through the brush, long, jet hair glistening in a glint of moonlight. He put the Colt down, rose on one knee, and wiggled a low branch, and she heard the sound and turned at once. He waited until she found him. She halted before him in her white shirt and black skirt, her black eyes moving over his body.

"You come to try more convincing, you can turn around," Fargo said gruffly. "I've nothing more to say on it."

"Didn't come for that," she answered. "Didn't come for fancy words such as integrity, either."

"You using my words, Alanna?" he asked, and the smile was in his voice.

"I guess so," she said gravely, her eyes very round.

"Guessing isn't good enough."

"All right, damn you," Alanna whispered, and her

arms came up, encircling his neck, and she pressed her lips to his. "No guessing," she murmured. "Wanting, just wanting."

He pulled her closer, one hand curled around the small of her back, and felt the softness of her breasts against him. Her lips worked against his, opening for him, the sweet pressure of silent promise. His hand went to the top of her shirt and moved down and the shirt buttons came open at once. He pushed the shirt from very white, very round shoulders as he pulled her down to the bedroll, and under the pale moon the longish breasts curved slowly and gracefully down to rounded cups, each tipped by a small, dark pink nipple in the exact center of a circle of lighter pink. A flat abdomen pulsated just below the gracefully long breasts and Fargo's hand pushed the riding skirt down and the snaps came undone. A pink petticoat slid down with the skirt and he enjoyed the loveliness of a small waist that slid into narrow hips, a flat belly between, and below it, a triangle as jet-black as her raven hair, curly and wiry, with tiny strands against her thighs. She had graceful legs with long, smooth thighs half-turned away together and Fargo brought his palm down atop the jet triangle. He felt the small pubic mound underneath already swelling, firm and warm against his palm.

His mouth came down to enclose itself around one of the long breasts and he pulled gently on the firm, pink nipple, sucked the breast deep into his mouth, and then circled the tender areola with his tongue. "Uuuuh," Alanna gasped. "Oh, oh . . . uuuuh." He let his tongue trace a slow circle and Alanna's gasps became whispered growls and he felt her hands digging into his back. His hand moved carefully down across the flat belly and over the jet triangle and his fingers pushed through the wiry tendrils, pressing down on the pubic mound.

"Oh, God, oh . . . oh, God," Alanna murmured,

but the long, smooth thighs still stayed pressed against each other. Fargo's lips pressed down on her mouth and he let his tongue dart forward, quick motions, in and out, each a small harbinger of greater pleasures. "Mmmmm, ah . . . mmmmmm," Alanna murmured, and he felt her lips contracting against his darting tongue.

His hand moved to the very point of the dense, raven triangle, and pushed down against the soft flesh of her thighs. "No, oh, oh . . . no, no . . ." Alanna gasped even as she pushed his face onto the long, graceful breasts. But his hand stayed, gently increasing its pressure, and he felt her thighs half-open, and suddenly he reached down to touch the dark moistness just below the triangle. "Ah . . . iiieeee . . . ah," Alanna cried out; her smooth thighs fell open and his hand pressed between her legs, cupping the warm wetness of her, and he herd her sharp intake of breath as she quivered for an instant.

His hand pushed into her dark and private portal and touched the edge of its wetness, coming to rest against the soft, pliant lips. "Oh, oh, no . . . oh, oh," Alanna breathed, and her thighs came together to trap his hand there as he felt the sensations coursing through her body. He pressed in farther, touched, and caressed and Alanna's thighs seemed to fly apart and her pelvis thrust forward as she screamed in pleasure. Her hands against his back pushed with newfound strength, and garbled, wordless sounds fell from her lips. He came over her, his hot, throbbing organ pressed atop the jet triangle.

"Uuuuuh . . . aaaagh . . . come . . . come to me, oh, God, come to me," she murmured, and her narrow hips moved, rotated, and searched for the ecstasy that lay so close. He pulled back, lifted, and came down upon her. He found her openness and pushed forward, sweet immersion, tender touch against answering tenderness, the ecstasy of flesh. Alanna's mouth opened, the veins in her throat bulging until her scream finally erupted, rapture given voice, and he felt her hands pressing hard against his back.

The longish breasts swayed back and forth as Alanna lifted and heaved with his every thrust and her raven locks tossed wildly from side to side. "God, oh, God," she managed to gasp, and her thighs slapped hard against his hips and he felt her scream before he heard it, the muscles of her belly growing taut against him, her back arching. "Now . . . now . . . iiiieeee," Alanna shrieked, and Fargo let himself come with her as her climax swept through her, halting the world as all the sensations of the flesh came together and he heard his own groan as her pulsating caress flowed around him. Finally, with a quick, shuddering cry, she fell back in the exhaustion of ecstasy and he lay beside her slender, narrow-hipped loveliness. She turned on her side and pulled herself up along his muscled body until she could press one breast against his face as she cradled his head with both arms.

He nuzzled the soft, long curve and let his tongue come forward to lick the pink tip and Alanna's arms tightened around his head. Finally she slid back down to rest her face against his chest. "It was more wonderful than I expected," she murmured.

"When did you start?" Fargo asked.

"Start what?"

"Wanting," he said.

Alanna pushed up on her elbows and a furrow touched her brow. "I asked myself that," she said. "Didn't come up with an answer. It's hard to know when wanting starts. I think it grows out of other things."

"Such as being grateful?" Fargo smiled

"That, and being impressed, being touched in some special way, suddenly caring, admiring, whatever," she said. "But it comes, it happens, that's all that

134

counts.'' She leaned forward and her mouth came over his.

''That's all that counts,'' he repeated as he pulled her down over him, the longish breasts flattening softly against his muscled chest, and as his hand stroked the small of her back, he felt the tiny, dark pink nipples grow firm again. He took her again, and Alanna's raven hair again tossed wildly when her final scream of pleasure rose to be muffled against his chest. Later, when she lay against him, letting her breath return, he enjoyed the feel of her long slender body, the tight rear, and the smooth-thighed legs. She rose when the moon hung low in the sky and reluctantly began to dress.

''It'd be best if I were at camp when the others wake,'' she said almost apologetically. When she finished dressing she stood against him for a moment longer, her hands moving down the smooth firmness of his chest. ''I haven't changed my mind about anything else,'' she said.

''Didn't expect you would,'' Fargo said.

She reached up and brushed her lips against his. ''Maybe we'll find another night.''

''Let's try,'' Fargo said, smiling, and she hurried away, disappearing into the darkness toward the hollow where the wagons were camped. Fargo returned to his bedroll and let sleep come quickly until the morning sun filtered through the trees to wake him. He walked to the hollow and found everyone up and ready to roll on.

Elsa and Eva watched him saddle up and he caught the curiosity in their faces and finally Eva sidled up as he finished tightening the cinch.

''Sleep well last night?'' she inquired, her round-cheeked face freshly scrubbed.

''You concerned or nosy?'' Fargo asked.

She shrugged and allowed a tiny giggle. ''Elsa and I saw the general's daughter walking around last night. We were just wondering.''

"Keep wondering," Fargo said.

"Did Sally ever come visit you?" Eva pressed.

"Keep wondering," he repeated, and drew a sly smile as the girls walked back to the Owensboro, apple-breasts bouncing. He pulled himself onto the pinto, nodded to Alanna as he passed, and waved the wagons out of the hollow.

The trail remained winding but it continued south and it rose gradually until he realized that he was moving through high mountain land. Riding a good distance ahead of the wagons, he paused where the trail branched off in two directions and he chose the one that moved slowly downward, glanced back to make sure the prints of his horse were easy to follow.

He rode on and saw the character of the terrain change. There were more rock formations, the soil grow drier, and gambel oak replaced the spruce. He'd seen no sign of Indian activity. When he rounded the edge of a tall sandstone crag, he pulled to a halt. Partway up the side of a wall of sandstone he spotted two pack mules, a pair of horses, and two men wielding pickaxes.

They halted the moment he came into sight, and picked up rifles lying on the ground.

"Easy does it, friends," Fargo said, and slowly steered the Ovaro up the narrow path along the sandstone. "Got six wagons coming along behind me."

"Wagons? Up here? You plumb crazy, mister?" one of the men said, a bearded man with a wide-brimmed hat that somehow managed to shield his face from the sun despite the holes in it.

"Strictly orders," Fargo said. "And against my advice."

"Then somebody else is crazy," the second man said. He had a long face partly covered with sandstone dust.

"Agreed," Fargo said. "Seen any Chiricahua?"

"Not lately," the first man said. "I'm Zeb Willis. This is Tom Huntson."

"Fargo . . . Skye Fargo," the big man answered.

"Fargo? The Trailsman?" Zeb Willis asked.

"Fraid so." Fargo smiled. "You've a good memory for names?"

"Used to work for Tim Greenspun. You broke trail for him more'n once."

"I did," Fargo said, and felt a stab of excitement push at him. "If you worked for Tim, maybe you knew a friend of his named Jamison."

"Bill Jamison? Sure did," Zeb answered.

"I was told he and his wife came up here prospecting for precious stones and gold and they disappeared. Maybe you know something about that," Fargo said.

Zeb Willis frowned. "Never heard of Bill Jamison going prospecting."

"His daughter and her cousins are in one of the wagons coming along behind me. They've come trying to find him," Fargo said, and the man's frown deepened.

"Can't be," Zeb answered. "Bill Jamison never had a daughter. He never had any kids. He and his missus stayed clear of other people's kids, too." The man's words danced in the air and hung there mockingly.

Fargo carefully framed his question. "You real sure about that, Willis?" he asked.

"Sure I'm sure," Zeb Willis said indignantly. "Hell, I worked alongside Bill Jamison for years. I ought to know."

"Doesn't seem likely there'd be another Bill Jamison that was a friend of Tim Greenspun," Fargo murmured.

" 'Course not," Zeb Willis said. "Somebody's fed you a crock of steer shit, boy."

Fargo's jaw muscle throbbed as he answered. "Seems so," he muttered, his lips hardly moving. "Much obliged."

When he saw the first dray come into sight on the road below, the general and Alanna riding alongside the team, Fargo took the pinto down to the road, pulled to the side as the wagons passed, and moved forward when Sally came along with the Conestoga. He saw her glance go up to the prospectors up on the sandstone hill. "I rode up and asked about your folks," he said evenly.

She looked at him with wide-eyed excitement. "They know anything?" she asked, and he saw Elsa and Eva leaning forward from their wagon to listen.

"Nothing to help you," Fargo said.

She let her face fall in dismay and Fargo felt the anger swirling inside of himself. She was a damn good actress, he swore silently. "Not even a lead? Nothing?" Sally asked.

"Nothing," Fargo said, and she allowed an unhappy shrug.

"We'll just have to go on till we find something," Sally said.

Fargo nodded and turned the Ovaro away. He trotted past the line of wagons and rode on ahead, his thoughts racing and each laced with cold anger. Little bitch, he murmured. Three little bitches. But why? He frowned. What were they doing here? Why had Sally Jamison lied, threatened, and cajoled her way into joining the general's wagons? There had to be some damn good reason for the three young women to risk their necks in these wild, Apache-infested mountains. His thoughts continued to race but he came up with no answers. He knew one thing though: Sally had been the first to lie to him. She was the key to Eva and Elsa being here and he was damn well going to get the truth, he promised himself.

8

As the day neared an end, the trail grew rocky again, but it continued its slow way downward. The Sangre range divided itself into two sections, the top one out of Colorado flattening down into low, rolling hills just before the New Mexico border. The bottom section rose again steeply in New Mexico to go farther south all the way beyond Santa Fe. They were heading down out of the top section, he realized. Another day and they'd be across the New Mexico border and he could turn left through the lower hills for Cimarron. If nothing else happened, the general could consider himself a lucky man, Fargo reflected, and spied a flat area bordered by gambel oak. He walked the pinto into the area, dismounted, and waved the first of the wagons in when they rolled into sight. One of Roscoe's men had managed to bring down two black-tailed jackrabbits and a fire was started at once.

Fargo relaxed to one side, watching Sally, Eva, and Elsa as they held quiet conversations with three of Roscoe's men. When the rabbits were finished, he took a portion.

Alanna came to sit with him, holding her plate on her knees. "I could find you again tonight," she murmured.

"Not tonight," he said more gruffly than he'd intended, and drew a questioning glance from the round, black eyes.

"You've someplace to go?" she asked, an edge in

her tone. "Or should I say someone else to see?" she added, the edge growing sharper.

"Might be, but not the way you're thinking," Fargo answered quietly.

"Of course not. You're going to discuss philosophy," Alanna snapped.

"You could say that," Fargo returned, and she rose, her lovely face set tight, and stalked away on sharp, angry steps. "Jealousy isn't good for you," Fargo said.

"Neither is tomcatting," she flung back without turning, and Fargo shrugged and wondered if possessiveness was a built-in part of her or just the result of her torn emotions.

He sat back and waited, letting the night deepen, and when the camp had settled down, he moved toward the Conestoga on silent steps. He had watched the wagon and saw Sally toss out tub water only a short while back. She wouldn't be hard asleep yet, he was certain and he slipped in through the front flap.

She sat up at once, bare-shouldered in a nightgown, and stared at him in surprise. "Fargo! What do you want here?" She frowned.

"You."

"Not here, for God's sake," Sally protested.

"Don't get your hopes up, honey," Fargo growled, and his hand shot out, closed around the top of the nightgown, and yanked her to him. "I'm here for answers, not ass," he said, his voice cold steel. "I want the truth and I'll damn well get it. You're not Sally Jamison."

He saw her eyes narrow for an instant but she was quick to draw indignation around herself. "Of course I am. What are you talking about?" she asked.

His hand tightened around the nightdress and he shook her hard enough to make her head snap back and forth. "Truth, that's what I'm talking about. Truth, dammit. Will Jamison never had any kids. One of those propectors knew him well. Now you tell me who you are or I'll take you and make you a present for the Mescalero.''

"You wouldn't do that," she said, but he caught the edge of uncertainty in her voice.

"Hell, I wouldn't. Being suckered makes me real mad," Fargo said. She blinked, swallowed but still held back. "Your right name. Start with that.''

She met his eyes and saw his icy anger and her shoulders dropped as she let out a deep breath. "Sally Hall,'' she muttered.

Fargo released his grip on the nightgown and she pulled it back over her small breasts with unnecessary propriety. "Eva and Elsa?" he growled.

"Eva and Elsa Turner.''

"Why the big act? What in hell are you doing here?'' Fargo demanded.

"The army sent us," Sally said.

"What?" Fargo exploded, unsure if he had heard right.

"The army sent us,'' she repeated, and he felt a wave of astonishment sweep through him.

"You trying to get out of one lie with another?'' he accused.

"No,'' Sally said indignantly.

"I believed one story of yours. I'm not about to swallow this one,'' Fargo threw back.

She reached over, turned up a small kerosene lamp, and began to rummage through a deep, cloth bag. She reached one arm all the way to the bottom of the bag and finally drew out a folded piece of paper. She pushed it at him, and he took it and leaned closer to the lamp with it. He felt the frown pressing hard into his brow as he read the strong handwriting on the piece of paper.

> Please know that Miss Sally Hall and Misses Elsa Turner and Eva Turner are on special assignment for the United States Government.
> General Maxwell Trammer
> U.S. Army, 5th Field Division

Fargo stared at the piece of paper, read it again, and felt only incredulousness churning inside him. "Godamn," he muttered. "You're a government agent." He lifted his glance to her as she shrugged.

"Sort of, but for this only."

"What's that mean?" He frowned.

"We were drafted, you could say," Sally replied, and he snapped out with impatient anger.

"Stop talking in riddles."

"It was like this," she began. "Elsa, Eva, and I were part of a small, traveling circus. We had a trick riding act. Eva and Elsa are both wonderful riders. The circus usually played near army bases, and Elsa, Eva, and I had our own thing going on the side." She paused and Fargo's stare questioned. "They'd make a pitch for an officer . . . We only went for officers. He'd sneak away to meet them and I'd come in at the right moment and catch them."

"And he paid up to keep you quiet and save his reputation and his career."

"Never failed. We even got a visiting congressman once." Sally smiled in fond reminiscence. "We were making real money but the army got mad, maybe because we were hitting too many high officers at too many bases."

"They've no appreciation for honest work," Fargo cut in. "They caught up to you and trapped you at your own game, I'd guess."

"That's just what they did," Sally said with almost a pout. "They sentenced us to fifteen years each, said they wanted to make an example of us."

"So how did all that bring you here?" Fargo queried.

"They needed help and we were told that if we did a job for them our sentences would be lifted."

"The job was to join the general's wagon train," Fargo supplied, and she nodded.

"The government has information that he's going

into New Mexico to set up a separate state with himself as president and they want him stopped," Sally told him.

Fargo heard the bitterness in his words. "She was right," he grunted.

"Who?"

"Alanna. She told me that was his real reason for the trip," Fargo said.

"The army also had advice that he was bringing down the money needed to set off his operation. Our job was to join with his wagons, go along and keep watching until we found out where he had the money or if he was picking it up or whatever. We were insurance, you might say, in case they didn't stop him themselves."

"Captain Oster's platoon was out looking for him," Fargo commented.

"That's right."

"That explains why he didn't search your wagons. He wasn't sloppy. He knew who you were," Fargo continued, and she nodded. "Your story was all to get me to help you join the general's wagons. How'd you find out I knew Tim Greenspun?"

"The general made no secret that he'd sent for you, so we asked around about you. Tim Greenspun's name came up. So did Will Jamison's."

Fargo shook his head. Incredulousness had turned to mere amazement. "But one thing hasn't changed," he said. "The general's not carrying any money. You've been watching. Two searches and nothing."

"I know." Sally frowned. "Makes me think maybe their information was all wrong."

Fargo turned, started for the flap of the wagon, and paused to frown back at her. "What if you'd found out something? What were you supposed to do about it?" he asked.

"There's a platoon waiting just east of Alamosa and another one south of Fort Garland. I told you that Eva

143

and Elsa are great riders. They were to go by night and race to whatever platoon was nearest. They'd take different routes just to play safe," Sally said. "I was to stay on and say we'd had a fight and they'd left."

Fargo nodded. Everything had been planned out as much as possible. "What do you do now? We're getting close to the New Mexico border," Fargo asked.

"We stick with him as long as we can. Those are our orders. Maybe he set this all up as a decoy. Maybe the money's coming in some other way," Sally suggested.

Fargo considered the idea. It was certainly a possibility but something bothered him about it. "He's been too nervous, too concerned with his damn wagons," Fargo said. "And I don't think he'd be risking his neck this much just to be a decoy. There's got to be something else. Don't ask me what."

He slid through the flap and hopped down to the ground. He surveyed the silent campsite and slowly walked toward the Ovaro. He saw one of the prone forms turn, turn again, and he caught the glint of jet locks in the moonlight. He changed directions and walked toward Alanna, who sat up, her eyes narrowed on him.

"Back so soon?" she slid at him. "She say no?"

"Get up and hold your damn tongue," Fargo said gruffly, reaching down and pulling her to her feet. She wore a short nightshirt of a gauzy material that rested lightly against her longish breasts, and he led her away from the other sleeping figures. He stopped inside the dark of the trees to face her. "You said I'd be apologizing to you," he told her, and watched her eyes grow wide.

"What'd you find out?" Alanna asked.

"Not important. But you were right."

She reached up, her arms circling his neck. "Thank you for saying so. Many men wouldn't," she said, and her lips touched his, soft, sweet pressure. "Now you'll stop him," she said, pulling back. When he made no reply, her frown came at once. "You have to."

"I don't know that it's any of my business," Fargo said. "I told you, a man's got a right to make his own mistakes."

"Your own government wants him stopped."

"That's up to them to do," Fargo countered.

"He lied to you about the job."

Fargo's lips pursed. "Now you're getting closer to home," he allowed.

"And I want him alive, not in prison or killed. Stop him for me, Fargo," she said, and her arms came around his neck again.

"Even closer," he murmured, and her mouth pressed hard onto his.

"Thank you," she murmured.

"You keep forgetting one thing. Stop him from what?" Fargo said. "Taking oil shale into New Mexico? That's no crime."

She looked away and there was frustration in her shrug. "He's doing more. I don't know how, but he is."

"I'll work on it. Meanwhile, you get some sleep," he told her. He patted her tight rear with one hand and she walked away, her face grave.

Fargo waited till she lay down on her blanket before he took his things and settled against an oak. He let thoughts drift through his mind. The wagons had been emptied, searched, the floors broken into and examined, and there'd been nothing. But Alanna's words returned. There was more, somehow, someway, there was more. Each time Morton Taylor had repaired and relocated and gone on, a man driven by something. Yet try as he did, Fargo found no answers, no insight, no flashes of brilliance to put everything in place, and he finally shut off the parade of unfruitful ponderings and went to sleep.

The next morning he rose early, exchanged glances with

Sally, and saddled the pinto. Eva and Elsa tossed him their bright smiles. They were still playing their roles for him. Sally hadn't had a chance to tell them not to bother, and he thought of the night they'd visited him. Sally's admission explained their enthusiastic expertness, he sniffed inwardly and swung onto the horse.

When the wagons rolled forward he stayed near while they carefully negotiated the steep, rocky path and he watched the nervous apprehension in the general's face. When they'd gone by the worst of it and the trail leveled out, he sent the pinto into a trot and rode on ahead. The land rose again and the trail wound past flat stone ledges that dropped off sharply. There was only one passage for the wagons to take and he increased his pace and rode on, turning from the trail to climb a hillside of gambel oak and pulling to a halt at the top of it.

His lake-blue eyes grew narrow as he peered into the distance to where a long line of foliage moved and a dust cloud rose into the air. No Chiricahua, he muttered to himself. Too much dust for Indian ponies. These were mounts wearing shoes, and he watched them cross to the right, then circle and cross back the way they'd come only a few hundred yards closer. He cast an eye up at the sun. It had already gone well into the afternoon sky, he took note, and he sent the Ovaro down the slope to meet the wagons as they came into view.

"Stay on the trail. I'm going on to have a closer look at some company in the distance," Fargo told the general, and hurried away. He put the pinto into a gallop until he'd covered a good distance and the sun was beginning to slide toward the horizon line. He pulled up onto a ledge and saw the line of horsemen a lot closer and halted to watch as they swept one way and then doubled back the other.

As he watched in the lowering light, he saw the riders come to a halt, the dust spiral end and the foliage settle into quietness. They had decided to make camp.

146

Fargo sent the Ovaro forward at a walk, crossed a dip in the terrain, then rose and finally he was in sight of the horsemen themselves. He gazed out from behind a pair of heavy-leafed oaks and made a quick count that gave him twenty-five men, perhaps thirty. He grimaced. He had a grand total of eleven guns at his command and his eyes narowed again as they peered across the distance. He took in the men as they made camp, scanned their clothing, and watched the one that was obviously their leader move among them.

Finally, satisfied with what he had seen, he turned the Ovaro and slowly moved away, stretching into a gallop when he had put some distance between himself and the horsemen. He rode hard through the dusk and reached the wagons with only a few minutes of daylight left.

"I think somebody else is looking for you, General," Fargo said.

"Who?" Morton Taylor asked.

"Don't know." Fargo shrugged. "But they're not just riding across the hills. They were making wide sweeps, the kind a posse makes when they're hunting."

"You find any other trails we can take?" the general asked.

"No, you're stuck with this one. But I saw something else, the lower end of the Purgatoire River. That means you could be crossing into New Mexico come morning," Fargo said.

"Good. Good," Morton Taylor muttered. "Let's make camp right here and get an early start tomorrow."

"This is as good a place as any for now," Fargo said, and turned away. He pulled the Ovaro to the side in the new darkness, and as the others began to settle down for the night, he slid his way to the Conestoga. Sally, tying a loose string on the canvas top, saw him approach and turned to face him. "Tell them to ride tonight," Fargo said.

"What?" Sally frowned.

"Elsa and Eva," he said. "Tell them to bring those platoons on the double."

"You find out what he's doing?" Sally asked.

"No, but if they don't bring those platoons back, there's good chance none of us will ever find out anything," Fargo said, and she heard the grimness in his voice.

"They'll ride," she said, and he hurried away. He settled down a few yards off the trail, and as the moon rose, he could make out Alanna's figure as she turned restlessly on her blanket. She'd been right all along, he snorted bitterly, but there was still no proof of it. Only, by tomorrow proof wouldn't really matter anymore. The harsh realities of events already set in motion would dictate the results. He closed his eyes, all too aware that there was little he could do to delay what he was certain was about to happen, turned on his side, and went to sleep.

He woke before the dawn came, rose, checked the Colt at his side and the big Sharps in the sadle holster, and moved silently to where the general lay. He put a hand on the man's shoulder and Morton Taylor snapped awake, blinked, and pushed himself to his feet.

"What is it?" the general asked.

"Last-chance time," Fargo said. "There'll be some thirty riders finding us tomorrow. There's no way to avoid them. You can leave the damn wagons and be alive to talk about it some winter night, or you can stay and get yourself killed."

"I'm not leaving my wagons, not after all this, not when I'm so close," Morton Taylor said.

"You wouldn't be the first man to give up his dreams," Fargo said. "I know why you're going into New Mexico."

148

The general's face composed itself into blackness. "I told you why I'm going."

Fargo looked up at the first streaks of dawn that crossed the mountaintops. "Suit yourself," he said, and walked away.

The others woke in minutes and were ready to roll on before the hour passed. Fargo glanced back to see the Owensboro hitched to the back of the Conestoga and two of the horses missing. But the general and the others were too intent on their own doings to notice, and Fargo sent the pinto on, followed the trail, and halted when the line of riders moved across to bisect the trail. Beyond, the low, flatter hills opened up and he turned as the riders swung onto the trail. He rode fast and returned to the others. He exchanged a quick glance with Alanna and saw the fear in her eyes. He swung in beside her, the general on the other side, and watched the spiral of dust coming toward them.

They reined up as the riders came into sight, a column two abreast and led by a tall, thin man. The horsemen reined up as they neared the first of the wagons, and Fargo's eyes swept the leader again. The man wore crossed gun belts over his chest, a Mexican *sombrero*, and two guns. Fargo's eyes swept across the others. They all wore almost the same outfits, but some had on the flat *poblanos* and a few had bandannas around their heads. The tall thin leader took in the line of wagons and raised his hand. "No trouble, *amigos*, and nobody gets hurt," he said.

"Who are you?" Morton Taylor barked.

"*Bandoleros, señor,*" the man said, and his eyes went to Fargo as he saw the chiding smile cross the big man's face.

"Shit you are," Fargo said through the smile, and the man's face darkened at once.

"Have you never seen *bandoleros* before?" the man asked, frowning severely. "I am Carlos Renado."

"Oh, I have, and you sure look the part, but you're no *bandoleros*," Fargo said.

The man's eyes hardened.

"You are *loco, señor.*"

"Not *loco*, just bright-eyed." Fargo smiled again. "*Bandoleros* don't ride in straight columns of two. I saw you make camp last night. *Bandoleros* tie their horses anywhere or in a loose circle. Yours were tied up in a single row in proper military formation. You're a Mexican army detachment all dressed up to look like *bandoleros*."

He heard Alanna's sharp gasp of dismay and watched the Mexican's eyes stay on him. "Perhaps you are, what you said, too bright-eyed, *señor*," the man rasped.

Fargo shrugged. "That's what I do best." He studied the man a moment more. "I'd guess it was Captain Renado."

The man acknowledged the remark with a nod of his head and allowed a thin smile to cross his face. "Step away from the wagons," Renado ordered, and with precision, his men produced short-barreled carbines.

"There's nothing but oil shale in the wagons," the general said. "You're wasting your time."

"He's right there. They've all been emptied and searched twice," Fargo added.

"Not the way I will," the Mexican said, and barked an order to his men. One came forward with a packhorse. Half of the detachment dismounted and began to take shovels and axes from the horse. Renado motioned to a flat rock in a clear space a dozen yards away. "Bring the wagons over there," he ordered, and his men climbed onto the wagons with quick precision and brought the four drays and Sally's wagons onto the ledge in a half-circle.

Fargo's eyes swept Morton Taylor and the others. Burt Roscoe and his men were quiet, all very aware

150

that to start a gunfight would be suicide. Alanna looked on with fear in her eyes and Sally's expression held more detached curiosity than anything else. Only the general's face twitched, his mouth a thin line.

Renado spoke to his men in Spanish and they began to unload the four drays, using their shovels to half-throw, half-push the shale onto the ground. They spread the rock after unloading it, and the captain watching carefully, they used their axes to smash open the larger pieces.

Fargo found himself nodding with approval. "Very thorough," he said to Alanna as her eyes found him. "They're making sure the big pieces aren't hollowed out and glued back together with bundles of cash in-side."

"Goddammit, you sound pleased about it," the general snapped, and Fargo smiled, his glance flicking up to the sun as it moved toward late morning.

"I always admire good work," he said. Especially the kind of thoroughness that used up precious hours, he added silently.

When the captain's men had finished smashing all the larger pieces of shale, they had nothing more than rubble but, Fargo noted, the sun had crossed into the afternoon sky.

"Bastards," the general muttered.

"Unhitch the wagons," the Mexican ordered, and his men obeyed, pulling all the horses to one side of the flat ledge. The captain spoke again in short, terse commands, and his men began to smash the wagons with their axes.

Fargo watched and exchanged a glance with Sally and she shrugged at the question in his eyes.

"No, you stop that, damn you," Taylor yelled, raced forward, and grabbed the upraised arm of one of the men as he was about to wield his ax. Another man smashed the general across the side of the head. Taylor went down, blood streaming from his temple and

151

Alanna cried out and rushed to her father. Burt Roscoe helped her pull the general back. "I'm all right," the general murmured as Alanna pressed a kerchief to his temple and helped him regain his feet.

Fargo watched Renado move his horse closer to the man. "You are *estupido,* General Taylor, a small man with big dreams. You have visions that you are that countryman of yours, Sam Houston, but you are not," he said. "But my country cannot take chances. The treaty's in effect and the monies we receive are too important to be jeaporized by a *plebeyo* like you." He turned away and barked at his men and they resumed smashing the wagons with their axes. They smashed the Conestoga and the Owensboro as well as the four drays, and when they were finished, the wagons were reduced to kindling wood. Only the wheels were left whole, some idly spinning on their sides.

The general, his head bandaged with a kerchief, glared up at the Mexican leader as the man rode up to him.

"What have you done with the money?" Renado asked.

"Nothing. There is none, goddamn you," Morton Taylor shouted, and Fargo saw Alanna throw a glance his way and he shrugged.

"Maybe you are bringing it in some other way," the captain said, and Fargo caught Sally's glance. He shrugged again but found himself wondering where the truth lay. He still couldn't accept the decoy explanation. Morton Taylor was too concerned to be running a decoy, even now with his entire operation destroyed. He still stared back at the Mexican leader with his hands clenching and unclenching and his eyes swept the kindling of his wagons with quick, nervous glances.

If it had all been a decoy, the game was over. There was nothing to do but recognize the fact. But there sure as hell were no bundles of money, Fargo grunted.

It was all as much of a strange question mark as when he'd started. But his thoughts snapped off at the Mexican captain's words.

"It doesn't matter," Renado said. "Because I must kill you, General. If you have the money coming in some other way, you will not be there to use it." He paused and his eyes swept the others and came to rest on Fargo. "And all the rest of you. I'm sure you understand that señor."

"Of course. That's no more than plain ordinary common sense," Fargo said agreeably. "You can't leave anybody alive who could say you were here."

"Exactly," Renado said, and turned his palms up in a gesture of helplessness. "It is a most regrettable set of circumstances."

"And we're all sorry about it, aren't we?" Fargo said. "Especially us."

"I cannot do anything else," the Mexican said.

"You can run," Fargo said, and the man frowned back. "That's right, run. You see, any minute now two platoons of U.S. cavalry are going to come charging up here. Now, you're members of the Mexican army deep in American soil. You know you're not supposed to be here. That's why you're all dressed up in those fake *bandolero* outfits as though you were on your way to a costume ball. If you're caught here on American soil, you know what that'll do to Mexican-American relations, don't you? There'll be treaties canceled and monies stopped and maybe more, and that's something your leaders can't afford."

Renado's lips pursed as he took in the big man's words. "What you say is true, of course, but I do not believe you about the cavalry platoons. I am not a fool, *señor*. You expect me to believe that two cavalry platoons would just appear here at this moment by coincidence?"

"No coincidence about it," Fargo said evenly.

"I see. You sent for them," Renado smiled.

"Bull's-eye," Fargo said.

"When?" the Mexican asked, and swept the others with a quick glance. "I have not seen anybody leave."

"You should've been here last night," Fargo said, and saw the man's eyes narrow again for a moment.

"A good try, *amigo,*" Renado said. "But we are wasting time." He half-turned to his men. "Line them up."

Fargo gave a half-shrug, started to turn away but spun back, the Colt in his hand, and fired in one quick, smooth motion. The single shot blew the sombrero from the captain's head and the rest of his men whirled, frozen for an instant. "The next one's right between your eyes, friend," Fargo growled.

The Mexican leader drew a deep sigh, but he was a cool, contained customer, Fargo saw.

"Very good shooting. *Excelente,*" he said. "I do not doubt for a moment you can put the next one right between my eyes."

"Then we understand each other," Fargo said, the Colt not moving a fraction.

"But I am a soldier, *señor,* on a mission. I am pre-pared to die for my country. You kill me and my men will open fire. The end result will still be the same. You will all die," Renado said, and Fargo cursed in-wardly. The man was indeed a trained soldier, a ded-icated officer, and by his code, he'd not show cowardice in front of his men. He'd not compromise, dammit, Fargo realized bitterly. Where was the god-damn cavalry? he cursed silently as he kept the Colt trained on the Mexican.

"Back off," he tried again. "Let my government take care of the general."

"We cannot take that chance," Renado said. "He is within a day of meeting with his friends. I have my orders."

Fargo cursed again silently. Then his wild-creature hearing picked up a sound, a low rumble that quickly turned into the pounding of hooves. "How's your hearing?" he asked the Mexican leader, and saw the frown slide over the man's face.

The sound of hoofbeats was clear now and a moment of panic seized Renado's eyes. Enough had died already on this dammed junket, Fargo murmured to himself. To start a gunfight and try to hold the Mexicans in place would be stupid. "Run, Captain," he said. "You know what it'll mean if you're caught here. By the time the platoon pulls up here you'll have maybe five minutes' head start."

The Mexican held a second more then wheeled his mount in a tight circle. He yelled commands at his men and they raced after him, in a proper column of twos, Fargo noted. He lowered the Colt and saw Alanna's eyes on him. She blew him a kiss with both hands and he looked beyond her to see the red-and-white platoon pennant come into sight. The cavalry unit raced to a halt and he saw Eva just a few paces behind a square-jawed lieutenant with some years on his face.

Fargo gestured to the debris that littered the ledge of rock. "Nothing worth bothering with here, as you can see," he said. "But there's a band of Mexican bandits hightailing it that way. Go after them. Stay on their tails till they cross the border."

"Will do," the lieutenant said, and motioned his troop forward.

Eva brought her horse over to Sally and stared at the littered ground. Fargo started to make a comment when he heard the thunder of hooves again, and he closed his mouth to wait. The second platoon arrived from the eastern side of the hills in a few minutes, Elsa riding beside a captain who reined to a halt and swept the litter with a frown.

"The other platoon's chasing a posse of *bandoleros*," Fargo said.

"I'm Captain Dillard," the officer said. "You can follow us back."

155

"Take me to Cimarron," Morton Taylor said, and the captain nodded. Alanna helped her father onto his horse and the remaining men fell in behind Burt Roscoe. Sally, Eva, and Elsa rode alonside Fargo.

"Nothing," he muttered. "Still nothing. The whole damn thing doesn't make any sense."

Sally shrugged. "We did our part, not exactly the way it was planned, but we did it. That's all that counts. We're off the hook. I don't really give a damn about the rest."

"Me neither," Eva said, and Elsa nodded agreement.

"You're free women again, then," Fargo said. "You going to go back to trick riding or riding tricks?"

"Riding," Sally said. "It's safer."

"Smart girls," Fargo agreed, and followed the troopers down a wide passage that led onto relatively flatland covered with dry grass.

Cimarron came into sight in another hour's ride and the captain pulled his troopers to a halt where a line of army tents stretched along one side of town. His gaze paused at Morton Taylor, swept past Alanna, and halted at Fargo. "I'd like to charge somebody with something but I don't have any grounds," Captain Dillard said.

"You don't," Fargo agreed. "We'll just be going our own way." The captain nodded and looked unhappy. Fargo waved to the three young women behind him and started to lead the Ovaro into town. Taylor and his men had huddled together and he saw the men were receiving pay vouchers as Alanna hurried over to him.

"There's an inn, the Cimarron Hotel. Father's staying there," she said. "I can't believe it's over. All this and nothing."

"I don't believe it, either," Fargo said.

"Even if he meets with his people, what'll it mean now?"

156

"Don't know, but something still isn't right," Fargo said. "The general is suddenly too goddamn calm. He's lost everything he said was so important, and he's calmer than he was throughout the trip."

"What are you going to do?"

"Walk away maybe," he said. "My part's done with. But something is still wrong."

"Wait till tomorrow to walk away, Fargo," Alanna said. "Maybe I'll walk with you then."

"Now that's a good reason for waiting." He grinned. "Till tomorrow." He strolled on and saw her hurry back to her father. But when he was out of sight, Fargo's eyes hardened. He didn't like being taken, lied to or hornswoggled, and he didn't like unfinished business. Morton Taylor was part of all four. None of it set right and it wasn't over, he was certain. He caught sight of the Cimarron Hotel and turned the Ovaro down a narrow space between two buildings almost directly across from it as the night began to descend over the town.

9

Fargo sat with his back against one of the buildings across from the hotel. The moon didn't reach into the narrow alleyway and he sat in pitch blackness, the Ovaro equally shrouded. The hotel was a busy place with lots of people coming and going, but as the midnight hour approached, it grew quiet and the streets of Cimarron were empty except for an ocassional horse and rider.

Fargo's eyes were on the entrance of the hotel when the familiar figure of the general emerged, two burly men following him. Fargo's stare took in the two men. They were new to him—neither had been at the ranch or on the trip. The general took his horse from a hitching post at the side of the hotel and swung into the saddle, and the two men did the same with their mounts. Fargo moved to the front of the alleyway, leaned out, and saw the three men riding on their way out of town. He had just swung onto the Ovaro when he spotted another figure hurrying from the hotel, black hair glistening in a shaft of moonlight, and he waited till she was on her horse and riding before he left the alleyway.

He hung back and let Alanna follow her father out of town and into the dry countryside. When the general started up a low hill where a stand of oak grew thick at one side, Alanna followed and Fargo grimaced and sent the Ovaro into a fast canter. He went into the trees, stayed there until he caught up to the girl, and swerved into the open to come alongside her. His hand reached out and clapped itself across her mouth as she spun in surprise. "Be quiet," he said, dropped his hand away, and led her to the edge of the trees. "You can't stay out in the open and follow this close," he said.

"What are you doing here?"

"Same thing you are. Great minds think alike," Fargo tossed out. "What in hell do you think you're going to do all by yourself?"

"Follow, watch, and maybe go get the army."

"Maybe?" he questioned.

"I don't want Father arrested and jailed," she said. "He had his own room at the inn and I watched and saw those two men visit him. You put the bee in my bonnet when you said you didn't believe it was over and that he was so calm."

"Didn't figure I'd have you along to look out for."

"I won't be in your way," she said. "I promise."

"What if it comes down to bottom line? What if I have to shoot Daddy?" he asked. "He's a determined man."

She paused for a moment. "Shoot low," she murmured, and fell silent.

He grunted and joined her in silence as they followed Morton Taylor and the two men back up into the low hills, across the rise of land, and still higher.

"He's going back to what's left of the wagons," Fargo said with surprise. He led Alanna across the trail to the other side where the land rose in a tree-covered slope, and by the hour's end they were approaching the flat ledge where the Mexicans had halted them.

"Dismount," Fargo whispered as he saw the general reach the flat ledge. He went forward on foot, Alanna beside him, and crept to where he could see the ledge. The three men had halted amid the litter of shale and smashed wood, and as he watched, one took a coil of rope from his pocket. Fargo's eyes fixed on the general as the man went to one of the wheels still on its side. He lifted it up and one man brought the rope to him while the other dragged another wheel across the ground.

"Goddamn," Fargo breathed as the men began to tie the wheels together with the rope. "The wheels. It's in the goddamn wheels."

"You can't hide money in wheels." Alanna frowned.

"No, not money, but something else just as good, maybe better," Fargo said. He pulled the Colt from its holster and aimed at one of the wheels lying half on its side against a broken axle. He fired two shots that blew splintered holes in the wheel. A cascade of something that might have been ground wheat poured from the holes. Only the wheat was a deep gold.

"Gold dust," Alanna breathed. "My God, gold dust inside the wheels."

"Four wagons, sixteen wheels, enough to finance any kind of operation," Fargo said, and ducked low as a hail of gunshots reverberated in the night.

"Up there," he heard Taylor shout. "Up by that rise."

Another hail of bullets plowed into the ground but Fargo rolled to one side, came up, and saw one of the men laying down a barrage while the other one tried to move up a slope and outflank him. He took aim, fired, and the figure half-spun and toppled backward down the slope. The other man spun and started to fire again, but Fargo ducked, rolled, and came up firing. The man started to rise, staggered, and fell to the ground. He twitched and lay still.

The general crouched beside the two wheels, a gun in his hand. "I'll kill you," he shouted into the night.

"Daddy," Alanna screamed. "Drop the gun. Please!"

160

Fargo saw the man's jaw drop open. "Alanna?" Morton Taylor cried.

She stood up so he could see her. "Yes, here, up here," she called.

"Dammit," Fargo muttered. Morton Taylor was a man obsessed, surrounded by shattered dreams, half-crazed with the tensions of a trip that had teetered on the edge of failure again and again.

"You've no right, Alanna," Taylor said, and stood up, the gun raised in his hand. "You've thrown in with them against your own father. You never did understand. I've got to do it. I've got to do it."

Fargo waited till the man lifted the gun a fraction higher and then the big Colt exploded in the pale moonlight. Morton Taylor screamed and clutched at his arm and his gun fell to the ground. The man staggered back and collapsed beside one of the wheels, and Fargo watched Alanna fly across the ledge to him. She tore the bottom of her skirt off to make a bandage around her father's arm as Fargo strolled to her, his face hard. He fired another shot at the nearest wheel; a stream of gold poured out at once and Morton Taylor groaned.

"Your friends back in Colorado supply you with this?" Fargo asked, and the man nodded. Fargo walked to the far edge of the rock ledge and peered down to see a steep clifflike drop. At the bottom moonlight glinted on a fast-moving river, one of the tributaries of the Rio Grande not that far to the west. Unhurriedly, the Trailsman dragged each wheel to the edge, put a bullet hole in it, and sent it rolling down the cliffside. The sound of splintering crash at the bottom had a musical ring to it, he decided.

"They won't miss it, but they won't give you any more," he said to Morton Taylor as the man watched with anguish. "As for your friends in New Mexico, they'll get tired of waiting and just go away."

When the last wheel crashed at the bottom, Fargo

lifted Taylor to his feet and Alanna held the man's arm. She helped him onto his horse and turned to face the big man with the lake-blue eyes. "The army will help you take him home," he told her, and she nodded.

"Thank you, Fargo," she murmured, and pressed her lips to his. "If you come by, I'll be waiting. And wanting."

"I'll remember that," Fargo said, and pulled himself onto the pinto. He fixed Morton Taylor with a long glance as the man sat with his head bowed on the horse.

"What are you thinking, Fargo?" Alanna asked.

"Sam Houston made the history books. He won't," he said. "I'm not sure who's the better for it."

Fargo rode away slowly, the Ovaro's hooves digging into the dry land of the territory of New Mexico, part of the American nation.

LOOKING FORWARD!

**The following is the opening
section from the next novel in the exciting
Trailsman series from Signet:**

THE TRAILSMAN #77
DEVIL'S DEN

*1860, where the northwest corner of Arkansas
borders Missouri, a land rife with unrest
where the lawless became the law. . . . . . .*

The big man blinked sleep from his lake-blue eyes
and the girl took shape in front of him, tall, a reddish
tinge to the brown hair that fell loosely around her
very attractive face—a face full of disdain. "Who the
hell are you, honey, and why'd you come busting into
my room?" Skye Fargo asked and grimaced at the
sour taste of too much bourbon coating his mouth.

"I'm not your bedmate of last night," the girl said
acidly.

"I know that," Fargo growled.

"How remarkable. Should I applaud?" she slid at
him. Fargo sat up straighter, the bedsheet barely covering his groin. It was too early and his head throbbed
too much for this kind of verbal sparring. He felt irritation balloon inside him.

"Guess I should've expected this," he said and her
frown questioned. "After the peach you get the pit,"
he growled and heard her angry hiss of breath.

"I'd laugh if I weren't so disappointed," she snapped.

"Then get the hell out of here and leave me alone," Fargo growled. "And knock next time."

"I did, six times," she said. "You're still too drunk to hear."

"Not drunk, honey, just having a little trouble waking up."

She spun on her heel, started for the door and paused beside the large porcelain basin of cold water atop the dresser. In one quick motion she scooped it up and flung its contents at him. He heard his own whoop of surprise as the icy water doused him. "Maybe this'll help you wake up," she tossed back and yanked the door open.

"Shit," Fargo swore, spit out water and swung his long legs over the edge of the bed. But she was gone, the door slammed behind her before he could even stand in his nakedness. "Goddamn little bitch," Fargo swore again and shook away the cold rivulets of water that ran down his body. He yanked the bedsheet up and used it to dry himself and then fell back across the bed, his long legs dangling onto the floor. "What the hell was she all about?" he asked aloud.

He let his thoughts unwind backwards, to the time when night had come and he'd played too long and too hard. He began at the start of it, to the thing that had brought him here to the town of Rockside. It wasn't the kind of job he normally took on, not even for the money offered him. Money doesn't do a man much good when he's full of lead and six feet under, he had told Marshal Sam Fogarty. But Fogarty, gray and wise as an old hoot owl, sent him to see Sarah Clenden, Fargo remembered, and he and Sarah sat down together with memories of old friends and old times. Her story had reached deep, as Sam Fogarty knew it would. Sarah and John Clenden had been old friends; Sarah, alone, deserved at least the hollow pleasure of knowing her husband had been avenged.

But still, Fargo remembered, he hadn't made any commitments, and Fogarty kept nudging him. Finally he agreed, and arrived in Rockside after breaking trail for a long and hot cattle drive all the way from Oklahoma. He was tired, dusty, hot and not yet ready to meet with Fogarty. The dance hall seemed the perfect spot to forget the world with strong whiskey and weak women.

So there had ben the bourbons, too many of them, and the girls, lots of girls, he remembered. But mostly there had been Fanny, young, new and anxious to please. He paused, recalling the parade of girls that had stopped at his table, frowning as he pressed his memory to recall faces and figures. None had been the tart-tongued package that had burst into his room. He couldn't remember having seen her anywhere before, not even during the short walk from the dance hall to the Rockside Hotel, where the rest of the night quickly became a thing of sweet heavings and twisting, tumbling bodies locked in desire. Again, he reviewed each moment until memory faded away in Fanny's embrace. There was nothing more until he'd been unceremoniously awakened. She'd been as good-looking as she was contemptuous. Fargo wasn't about to just forget her strange visit. Blowing a deep breath of air from his lungs, he rose, finished drying himself, donned trousers and found some fresh water in an adjoining room. Finally dressed, he went down the single flight of steps to where an elderly desk clerk looked up at him.

"That wild, raging girl that just stalked out of here," Fargo said, and the man nodded. "Why'd you let her up to my room?"

"First, she asked for you. Second, if we stopped every gal that went to a man's room we'd have no business and no hotel," the desk clerk said. "Besides, she's been comin' in here asking for you for the past three days.''

Fargo frowned at the clerk's words. ''She give a name?''

''Once. Melanie Harper,'' the man said. ''She's staying with the Ebersons just outside of town.''

''How do you know that?'' Fargo frowned.

''They came with her the first time and I heard them talking,'' the clerk said. Fargo noted the clerk's words and strolled from the hotel. Outside, he found the town crowded with long-haul wagons, some dead-axle drays, a number of heavy-geared mountain wagons and a sprinkling of one-horse farm wagons. He saw cargoes of barrels, kegs, lumber and grain sacks, plenty of riders leading pack mules and a few ten-mule salt teams. Rockside was plainly a town of commerce, a stop between the roads into north Missouri and west to Kansas and the southern routes into the Arkansas territory.

He ought to be heading to see Sam Fogarty, he knew. The marshal was waiting for him but there'd be time enough for that. There was always time to put one's neck in a noose. The Trailsman unhitched the Ovaro and led the horse to the public stable where he bought a sack of good oats and used the dandy brush and hoof pick from his saddle bag to remove caked dirt and mud from the animal's coat. He finished with the sweat scraper and stable rubber so that the striking horse's jet-black fore and hind-quarters and white mid-section fairly gleamed. He rode casually to the edge of town and saw the house there, a neatly fenced, two-story frame structure. He reined to a halt beside the sign stuck in the soil. *Eberson*, it read in neat letters and as he watched, the door opened and a man and woman emerged together, both slight-framed, dressed in dark, conservative clothes. ''Yes?'' the man inquired.

''Looking for Melanie Harper,'' Fargo said.

"I'm afraid she's not here at the moment," the man said.

Fargo scanned the couple without smiling. "Name's Fargo," he said. "Skye Fargo."

"Oh," the woman uttered and they glanced apprehensively at each other.

"Something wrong?" Fargo asked.

"Well, I'm afraid Melanie isn't interested in talking to you any longer, Mr. Fargo," the man said.

"Too damn bad. She came looking for me. Now I'm looking for her," Fargo snapped. "Where is she?"

The couple exchanged wary glances again and Fargo decided to press. "The longer it takes me to find her the madder I'm going to be."

"She's gone to hire somebody else," the woman said and sounded half apologetic. Fargo kept the smile inside himself. He didn't give a damn who she hired for what. He just had some unfinished business with her.

"Where?" he growled.

"The saloon in town," the man answered.

"Much obliged," Fargo said and turned the Ovaro away. He rode slowly, making his way through the town until he reached the saloon and winced as the too-recent memories rushed over him. He even imagined the taste of too much bourbon in his mouth as he dismounted and swore at himself. He slid through the double doors, against the wall, and edged into a chair in one corner. Two dozen or so men were in the room, half of them at the bar, the others scattered around the tables. Melanie Harper stood at the corner of the bar, very straight, almost with school-teacher primness.

He took her in carefully for the first time and saw a straight nose and a wide mouth with full lips, nice, high cheekbones, eyes that were a pale blue fire—strangely alive despite their paleness. A long, graceful neck went into square shoulders that were covered by a white shirt that rested on what seemed to be full-cupped breasts. A brown riding skirt swirled around long-lined thighs and one of the men broke into his appraisal with the question. "What do you call paying top dollar, honey?" the man asked.

"Believe me, it will be just that. But I want takers, first," she said. "I'll be honest with you. There will be danger, I'll tell you that now. I want somebody to take me into Devil's Den country."

Fargo scanned the room and saw the men glance at each other, some with a wry grunt, others with contempt. "Top dollar ain't gonna be enough for me, lady," one man said.

"Me neither," another put in. "Not to go to Devil's Den." A murmer of agreement traveled through the room and Fargo watched Melanie Harper show neither disappointment nor anger but only a cool firmness.

"The man I want must be able to trail. He must be skilled at reading signs in people and places," she said. "I'll pay whatever it takes, but I won't settle for less." She had an air of lecturing that he knew would irritate her listeners normally but in this instance they'd not be taking up her offer, anyway. Fargo's eyes slowly scanned the room again. The men were all ordinary cowheads at best, some drifters, a few with cracked leather boots that showed they were on hard times. He was surprised when the figure stood up across the room.

"I'm the man you want, little lady," the man said, and Fargo saw a tall figure wearing a light-tan stetson. Beneath the hat, he saw a lined face, a mouth that turned down at the corners. "I've broken trail all over the west," he heard the man say. "But I want to talk private, now. If I take a job, I don't want a lot of ears knowing everything about it."

She considered his words for a moment. "Fair enough," she agreed. "What's your name?"

"Shuler. Biff Shuler," the man said and Fargo's eyes narrowed on the tall figure. He scanned the man's face first and he saw eyes that moved restlessly back and forth, no keen sharpness in them at all and below the eyes, a face that wore hardness on the outside, only. Underneath, he saw cruelty, selfishness, and the lines of cunning. This wasn't a face that knew the lone contentment of the trail. The eyes held no sharp steadiness that could see where others couldn't. Fargo's gaze traveled down the rest of Shuler's figure and saw the worn leather belt, the holster with frayed straps. Biff Shuler couldn't trail his way through a chicken coop.

"Where do we talk in private?" Fargo heard Melanie Harper ask.

Shuler moved to stand close to her and Fargo saw her nod twice, answer the man in a low voice, and begin to stride out of the saloon. Fargo remained against the wall as the young woman walked on quick steps, chin held high and looking neither right nor left. As soon as she disapeared through the double doors, Fargo saw Shuler turn, motion, and a shorter man with a round, oily face hurried over to him. Both sat down at a far table, ordered another round of beers and talked in low voices Shuler interrupted from time to time with a harsh laugh.

Fargo stayed against the wall, nursed a bourbon and waited. He refused to speculate but he was certain of one thing. The man was a fraud and he'd more on his mind than taking a job he couldn't fill. Fargo was about to order another drink when Shuler rose, with the short man following. Fargo tossed a coin on the table and carefully followed the two men outside. He watched them take their horses and begin to ride from town. Staying back, he rode after them, falling back further as the two men took a road south out of town. They turned into a hackberry-covered hillside and left the road. Fargo moved through the trees, staying within easy earshot. The hill leveled out and a deer trail appeared. The two riders took it and Fargo drew a little closer and saw the shorter man suddenly swerve to the right, leave the deer trail and disappear into the thick foliage.

They were splitting up, Fargo noted and was all but certain why as he followed Shuler. He slowed down when the deer trail suddenly opened up onto a mountain pond, an almost perfect circle of clear, cold water amid the trees. Fargo saw Melanie Harper come into sight, standing near her horse almost at the edge of the pond, the sun highlighting the reddish tint in her flowing hair. Fargo halted, slid silently from the Ovaro and crept forward as he saw Shuler dismount before the girl. "Found it easily. Your directions were good," Fargo heard Melanie say. "Now that we're alone we can talk. You first."

"What's a fine-looking woman such as yourself want to go to Devil's Den for?" Shuler said, his eyes roaming up and down Melanie's body.

"I've my reasons. They're important only to me," she said. "Will you take me and can you?"

Fargo saw the anticipation in the smile that slid across Shuler's face. "I'm going to take you, little lady, but not to Devil's Den," he said. "I'm going to take you to bed." He started toward the girl and Fargo watched Melanie step backwards and reach into the brown skirt. She brought out a Remington-Rider pocket revolver, double-action five shot, more than powerful enough to kill a man at close range.

"Stay back," she warned and Shuler halted, surprise in his face. "I guess this is my day for disappointments," she said. "You're mistaken for taking me as a näive little fool."

Fargo's eyes had gone to the thick brush behind her and he watched as the lariat whirled out from the trees. Melanie caught the swish of air and tried to turn, but the loop came down around her and was yanked tight instantly. With her arms pinned to her sides, she nonetheless tried to whirl and bring the pocket pistol up but the lariat was pulled hard again and she went down, first on one knee and then yanked onto her face. Shuler was at her in one quick bound and yanked the gun from her fingers. He laughed as he threw it away.

"I guess you're the one who made the mistake, honey," he said and the shorter man with the lariat stepped from the trees and walked up to where the rope circled Melanie. His round, oily face had become a thing of shiny anticipation and he slid his tongue across his lips.

"Me first, Biff," he said.

"Like hell," Shuler answered and yanked Melanie to her feet, his eyes devouring her body. "Loosen the lariat so's we can get that shirt off her." The shorter man began to loosen the rope and Melanie tried to tear free of it, dropping down to whirl out of its grasp. Shuler let her almost succeed, then grabbed her by her loose, red-tinged brown hair and yanked back hard. The girl cried out in pain. She fell back against him and he brought one arm around, his hand folding her breasts. "Now, that's better," he slavered. "Christ, they're real nice and soft. Like new, Sonny," he chortled. Melanie twisted her neck around, and sank her teeth into his forearm.

"Bastard," Fargo heard her swear under the sound of Shuler's cry of pain. His hand dropped from her breasts as he pulled his arm back and again Melanie tried to twist away but this time the other man lashed out with a short, straight punch that caught the girl in the stomach and she went down with a gasp.

"Bitch," Shuler snarled. He reached down and yanked the girl back on her feet and again wrapped one arm around her, this time up close under her chin so she couldn't move her head as he cupped her breasts. Fargo, the Colt in his hand, started to step from the trees but halted. He had to wait for another moment, he swore silently. The way Shuler had hold of Melanie she was a perfect shield for him. Fargo remained in place as the man dragged her forward and suddenly flung her to the ground. He fell on top of her at once, pressing her hard into the soft earth at the edge of the pond. "Grab her arms," he yelled and the short one moved in a half-circle to place himself above the girl, seizing her arms as she tried to claw at her attacker. "Now we're going to have us some fun, bitch," Shuler said, one hand tearing the girl's shirt open and Fargo caught a flash of cream-white mounds as her slip ripped. Shuler took a moment more to yank his trouser buttons open when Fargo stepped from the trees.

"Put it back, mister, unless you just want to give it some air," he growled and saw Shuler freeze in place on top of the girl. The shorter one he had called "Sonny" looked up in surprise, but kept his grip on Melanie's wrists. "Throw your gun away, nice and easy," Fargo said and Shuler stared at him for a long moment. "I'm not going to tell you twice," Fargo said and the man slowly took his sixgun from its holster and tossed it a dozen feet away. Fargo's eyes flicked to the shorter man—a flash of ice-blue—and Sonny released Melanie's wrists, straightened up on his knees and took his gun out. He threw it in the other direction and Fargo took another step forward as Shuler pushed himself up from Melanie and the girl jumped to her feet. She backed away, halting at the edge of the pond, and looked on with her pale-fire eyes wide.

"What's she to you?" Shuler blurted out and moved a few paces closer to his horse.

"A pain in the ass," Fargo said and saw surprise touch the man's face. His gaze flicked from Shuler to Sonny and back again. "I hate to waste bullets," he said and Shuler frowned. "That's the only reason I don't put one in each of you," Fargo explained. "Get on your horses and ride while I'm still feeling frugal."

"You can't send us out without our guns. This damn country's full of Osage and Wichita. Besides, we don't have the money to buy new guns," Shuler protested.

Fargo moved quickly, scooped up Shuler's gun and emptied it, doing the same with the shorter man's revolver. "Take the bullets out of your gunbelts," he ordered and both men glowered as they obeyed. When they were finished he tossed their guns at their feet. "Now all you have to do is buy bullets at the next town," he said. Shuler and Sonny both bent down to retrieve their guns and Fargo allowed himself a glance at Melanie Harper. She still watched with her eyes wide. But the moment's glance was an indulgence and a mistake. He caught the movement out of the corner of his eye as Shuler, still bent over, threw his sixgun with a flat, underhand motion. Instinctively, Fargo twisted away and felt the gun hit him across the back of his left shoulder. He started to whirl back and saw the shorter man barreling at him in a running, half-flying dive. Fargo fired but his shot only grazed the top of the hunched-down figure and Sonny slammed into him at the knees.

Off-balance, Fargo felt himself go down hard and the Colt jar loose from his grip as he hit the ground. Sonny leaped sideways to grab the gun but Fargo managed a backhand blow that caught the man on the side of the head and knocked him aside. Fargo half-rose, saw the kick coming at him as Shuler stepped forward and he rolled just in time to avoid the blow. It was Shuler's moment to go for the Colt and as the man bent down to pick it up Fargo kicked out, using his hands for body support on the ground. The blow hit Shuler in the ribs and the man grunted in pain as he fell to one side. The moment was enough to let Fargo regain his feet. He moved forward and parried a wild right swing from Shuler, who was about to let a straight right go in return when he glimpsed the short figure coming at him from the side, head down, arms flailing. Fargo decided against delivering the blow to Shuler, which would have left him off balance and instead, brought his knee up sharply and felt

173

it crack against Sonny's jaw. The short figure went down with a groan of pain and Fargo ducked at once as Shuler sent a winging left and right at him.

Both blows missed and Fargo came up with a straight left delivered from a crouch, all the strength of his back and shoulder muscles behind it. The blow landed flush on Shuler's jaw and the man stopped in his tracks, staggered, and his eyes went blank for an instant. Fargo's right followed to land at the same place and Shuler spun in a full circle and collapsed into unconsciousness on the ground. The shorter man started to get up, and had reached his hands and knees when Fargo's fist came down to slam against the back of his neck. Sonny fell onto his face, twitched for a moment and lay still.

Fargo drew a deep breath, straightened up and crossed to where Melanie stood at the edge of the pond, her pale-fire eyes still round. She nodded as he approached, and the sun's last rays managed to glint on the reddish tint in her hair. "I guess I wasn't alert enough," she said.

Fargo moved in a single, sweeping motion, took another step forward and scooped her up in his arms. He tossed her in a half-circle and she hit the cold water with a resounding splash. "Maybe that'll help you be more alert," he said, spun on his heel and strode to the Ovaro. He was in the saddle when she came up blowing water from her mouth. Her breasts were nicely-cupped, he noted as the wet shirt clung to them revealingly.

"Wait! You bastard!" she shouted but he was riding away at a fast trot. He didn't look back. The two men would stay unconscious more than long enough for her to ride away, and he hurried through the trees as the day began to turn to dusk. He was curious about Melanie Harper, he admitted to himself, but it was a curiosity he'd happily put aside. She had all the earmarks

of being just what he'd told Shuler—a pain in the ass—
and he was about to have enough problems without
adding another. He put the Ovaro into a canter, heading for Rockside and Marshal Sam Fogarty.